DYING TO END IT

JOEY SANCHEZ

For my father.

You were always there for us, you always had our backs, and you never rolled your eyes when you heard,

"I know this is gonna sound crazy but…"

Also for my family.

I love you all.

CONTENTS

Prologue

The bickering of old married couples constituted the best possible Rorschach test to find out a person's worldview. For every seventy-year-old couple sniping at each other in the aisle of a grocery store over which brand of canned beans their eldest child—now in his forties—used to hate as a kid, there'd be three distinct types of onlookers with wildly differing responses.

The first would be the guy smugly laughing to himself, the one obnoxiously telling everyone he was smart enough to avoid marriage, didn't you know?

In fact, this one had a wise uncle take him aside as a young man to tell him all about how women just got uglier and fatter as they aged, their skin crinkling and their breasts reaching for their knees, and it was best not to get tied down by any of them since they were all the same.

So, he'd stayed single ever since, taking that bickering old couple as a sign he'd done right, a good distraction from the fact that he'd grown old, fat and saggy too, also going home alone.

The second onlooker would be the smiling young lady, the one burning in wistfulness. Well into her forties and with at least one divorce under her belt, she'd be pretty salty about it all, but still managed a warm smile at those old-timers. You see, fading beauty notwithstanding, she held out hope of someday still finding the one she'd been looking for, the one who would stay and argue about beans with her. To her, that old couple was the epitome of romantic love; they may well fight, but still held hands and went grocery shopping together, their only day out in a while.

The third was the guy or girl barely taking notice of anything going on around them because as far as they were concerned, bickering was a part of any relationship, good or bad, romantic or platonic, and who even cared anyway? Hell, there was a lot more to worry about than what other folks did; they had enough of their own issues to worry about, their own petty arguments too.

So, they'd just reach around the bickering couple, jostling to grab themselves their own can of beans, the brand the wife liked best, and off they went, casting a slight nod at the arguing old folks, just leaving 'em to it. Not that the old couple would have noticed that nod anyway.

"I could never get *my* girls to eat beans at all," Frank voiced to the couple, probably only ten years or so his senior. Yet in his head, they were *'old old',* like grandparents. But the wistful girl off to the left probably didn't see any age difference between them all. Such was life.

The old couple halted their bickering for a few seconds to turn and smile at him, nodding in a *this guy gets it* type of way. It looked as if he'd just made their day, acknowledging their beans.

Frank went on about his shopping, picking up the two or three more items his wife had asked him for. She'd already started making dinner—meatballs—only to realize she was short of a few ingredients, so an impromptu visit to the store was in order.

And as was always the way on any errand, Frank had to go along with her.

Or rather, she had to go along with Frank. Why, he couldn't fathom.

It was slightly odd how they both ventured out on this particular occasion since Bianca had to stay in the car on account of her twisted ankle. Why was she even here? Oh, but she wasn't happy about being 'grounded'; there was a 'system' to picking up groceries, she said, and she couldn't expect Frank to have it down pat. But the doctor had said to stay off it—the bad leg, that is—so Frank had to put his own foot down and wander into the store alone, system or no system.

In their thirty-five years of marriage, there wouldn't have been many things on which Frank hadn't needed to compromise a time or two. But this time, he could hardly hold a grudge, could he? Doctor's orders were doctor's orders. Shortly, he came back out of the store, and there she was, still sitting in the car of course, now busily applying lipstick in the visor mirror, stretching her mouth this way and that, smacking her pretty lips together, applying some more gloss.

He smiled and just stood there, knowing better than to approach while she was putting her face on. Even after all these years, she still insisted on getting up well before he did to put her makeup on and take out her curlers. He never asked her to do that either, certainly never demanded it. Wouldn't even have dared since Bianca was her own person.

But truth be told, he also liked that she did it, liked that he didn't have to walk around town with a wife who dressed as if she'd just rolled out of bed. His Bianca took pride in herself.

But his girls took issue with the effort she put in for some reason.

"Ma, you're almost sixty now. Who are you trying to impress? It's not for Pop, is it? Have you looked at him lately?” Daniella, their youngest child, had giggled as she said it but of course, she’d been the one to fire off that question, which made sense. Now in her third year of college, she was one of those women who wore her pajamas everywhere, insisting they were all the rage.

“Yoga pants aren’t pajamas, Pop! You are just *so* out of touch!”

She’d got so mad one time after he’d tried to tell her how to dress more like an adult. “You could do worse than take a leaf out of your ma’s book; she always looks after herself.”

Bianca had glowed with pride and love at his words. Daniella, however, hadn’t. Her face turned a mottled mix of pinks and purples like a can of chopped ham and pork.

Then she’d put him in his place, in no uncertain terms. Baggy pantsuits were *it,* he’d learned. Those ‘shapeless pajama things’—as he still called them—were what all the fashionable young women wore these days. But then he mused on it; sure, there was worse attire a young woman could be seen in. Skirts that were too short, for example. That’d never do, not for his girls.

So now, he’d stopped commenting on it in fear of pushing Daniella to rebel. God help him if she went for the short skirts in an act of getting her own back.

"Dad, it's a different world now to when you were growing up," said his elder girl, Annabella. And maybe it was, but that hardly mattered. In the 'old world' when Bianca had been young, she was always getting razzed about her outfits then too. Long, straight hair, no makeup, and no bras was the expected look, and Bianca wasn't having any of it.

He hadn't known her in high school, but he'd seen all the pictures. Skirt, blouse, and oxfords every day, while all her friends were wearing slacks.

She was her own kind of rebel then, and she still was one now. And he wouldn't have wanted her any other way. She knew who she was, and he liked it. No one could say she lacked esteem.

A lot of his friends from the neighborhood—well, the ones who were still kicking—got mad about what the world was like now, filling up their Facebook pages with all kinds of rants about the millennials and the government, waxing nostalgic as though the 1970s had been so great.

They hadn't been. So, Frank didn't spend a lot of time mad at what the world had become.

He had Bianca; she was his world, and that world was a mostly beautiful one.

Once she had folded the visor back up and put her lipstick away, Frank walked back to the car and dropped into the driver's seat, his back popping as he twisted to put the bags in the rear.

"Be easier if you put the bags in first, you know," Bianca said, giving him a smile. And she wore that expression that said she was right as usual. Some days, with all the advice she had to dish out to him, it was a wonder Frank ever survived a single day out and about on his own.

"Yeah, and it'd be easy to give the guy who owns the Jag next to us a heart attack when he sees my back door opening near his car," he remonstrated. It was a good point after all.

"That's not a Jag, that's a Caddy. One of the new ones."

He raised his eyebrows at her. She was really going to debate cars with him, was she?

With a *we'll see about that* expression, he pulled out of the parking spot. Not one to be cowed, Bianca gave him a, *yes, we certainly will* expression right back.

Once they were perpendicular to the mystery car, as one, they both turned to look out the passenger window; what kind of car had they been parked next to?

That was what they both sought to determine.

"What the hell is a Genesis?" Bianca asked, rolling the window down and sticking her head out to get a closer look.

"Haven't the foggiest idea," Frank answered. His face showed annoyance that he'd been wrong about the make of the car, but he was happy Bianca didn't get it right either. "We'll Google it when we get home. A nice-looking car, whatever it calls itself."

And off they went on the way home. Their route was a nice drive since the store was right off the highway exit and from there, it was a straight shot back to their neighborhood. Easy!

Well, it was *usually* a nice drive, put it that way. *Usually* easy.

Maybe not this time.

No sooner had Frank pulled out of the parking lot than the flashing of lights came up on them from behind. Red and blue, no less, and so many of them, all gathering right in front of the on-ramp to the highway. "Long line of cars backed up there," he voiced to Bianca.

"Well, why don't you—" she managed to get out.

"Take a left… do the only detour we can take," he finished for her.

She nodded with a knowing look as if still taking all the credit for their mutual idea.

Frank did not take the left though. Instead, he made a tactical decision on his own, turning right to take the surface streets. It would take usually longer winding his way through all these neighborhoods, but with that pile-up blocking the on-ramp, he'd probably still get home earlier.

Bianca either didn't mind or just didn't say anything, too busy digging around in that enormous 'organizer' purse of hers, so organized it had a pocket for everything.

Well, she could never remember which pocket held what, and there were a lot of them to rummage through. She was looking for something, her brow furrowed, deep sighs emanating.

He'd bought her a new purse last Christmas, a smaller one. But she had yet to use it. Here was an opportunity to make a point. One on which, hopefully, she might concede for a change.

"You know, you'd find what you're looking for a lot easier if you used the purse I got you."

Without looking up, she rolled her eyes. "Frankie, that purse wouldn't hold half of what I need it to. And there's nothing wrong with my pocketbook."

"Pocketbook, ha! It's the size of the kids' book bags. And you don't need half of what you lug around with you all the time either."

She shot him a withering stare. "Yeah, you always say that. Until you need cuticle scissors or a pencil or a magnifying glass, then you appreciate all I lug around, now, don't you? Besides, how would *you* know what I have in here? I do hope you haven't been looking at what I—"

"No, no. All your secrets are safe. It's more than my life is worth."

He laughed anyway, unable to argue with her on the point about her always managing to produce whatever it was he or the girls ever needed while out and about. There was no denying Bianca always had it. A tissue, a receipt, a magnet, a pair of forceps, a collapsible camping mug… and feminine hygiene products, even though Bianca didn't need them anymore. Whatever it was, she'd have a couple of them stashed away in that bag.

It was the Noah's Ark of women's accessories, safeguarding two of everything.

"What are you looking for, anyway?" he asked.

"The recipe for the meatballs. I want to make sure we have everything before we get home."

"Maybe we should have done that at the store?"

"Probably so, but *you* distracted me by going on about the car," she said.

She emitted a triumphant *a-ha!* Then she held up the index card.

Frank laughed and looked over at her, seeing the yellowed card with a flower doodled on its edges. One of the girls had probably drawn it at some point. It was in purple ink, so he'd guess it was Annabella. She'd gone through a long, almost pathological purple phase in her early teens.

He was about to say something about the blossom, glancing up at Bianca's face.

But those words never did get a chance to be freed into the air.

As if in a surreal slow motion, he watched his wife's complexion lose all color and her mouth fall out of its smile, assuming a horrified silent scream, eyes wide, knuckles white.

Too late, he whipped his eyes back to the road, seeing the grille of the truck barreling forward, then slamming, crumpling the hood, smashing his windshield.

The crash was so loud it would come to fill all his memories of that day, the impact like a gunshot, his body flung and smashed and crushed, left bleeding and horribly maimed.

And through it all, despite his own colossal injuries, he saw only Bianca's face… It had stretched and morphed in terror. And then—

Like still images, flashes in a slide show, those sights would haunt him for the rest of his life.

CHAPTER 1

One Year Later.

In the year he'd spent confined to his bed, Frank was starting to rethink his policy on not being angry with the modern world. Specifically, he was angry at that sexless son of a bitch who'd decided that nurses should swap out their crisp, universally flattering white dresses and nurse shoes for scrubs and Crocs. He didn't think much of that decision at all.

Even the sight of Samantha at the bedside did nothing to soften his view.

Of course, he'd hear her shuffling in his direction way before she actually appeared, and that was enough to get his back up. Those infernal beach shoes!

What had become of professional attire?

Samantha was his most recent nurse, the one responsible for him during the night hours. He'd gone through three, and every one of them *was* professional, *was* efficient, and *was*… well, condescending as hell, as if it were a pre-requisite for the job. They'd all start off the same way, blustering into his room—now with its unfetching hospital bed instead of the four-poster antique that he and Bianca had picked out before their wedding—and introducing themselves. Kind of.

Wasn't an introduction supposed to be a two-way thing? "Hi Mr. Vitale, I'm Samantha. I'm here to take care of you while your daughter sleeps. How does that feel? Good? Great."

They never did wait for an answer, no doubt used to seeing people laid up in bed as just another slab of useless lard about to pass into the next life. And their baby talk was the height of annoyance. "How are you today, sweetie pie, honey bun, my treasure, my gorgeous boy?"

Well, maybe not quite that bad but along those lines. Frank's neck would bristle at it daily.

Then there'd be the, "and you just let me know if there's something in particular you want me to do while I'm here."

Oh, there was plenty he wanted them to do, all right! He could always think of a couple dozen things! But that was where their selective hearing kicked in. It didn't matter if Frank said he needed the pillow fluffing or that the blanket straightening didn't feel so good, and the bedding was sliding off his clammy legs again.

No matter what he asked for, there was always a reason for not doing it.

Even the slightest thing seemed destined to become a battle of wills.

"Don't suppose you could close the curtains for me, could you? The sun hurts my eyes."

"Oh, sugar, you don't want to block out all that lovely sunshine. Think of your vitamin D. Besides, it's God's way of shining down His glory on you, reminding you He's still there for you and not letting you out of His sight. But before I go, is there anything else I can do for you?"

"Wouldn't mind a piece of that cake you picked up for me. The chocolate and cream…"

"Oh, Frankie, Frankie, Frankie. You and your cake. It'll be the death of you, will cake!"

"Just a tiny piece. It'll be past its *best before* date soon. And besides, it'll hardly see me off; there are millions of people walking around who've been eating chocolate cake. As far as I know, they're still breathing. Some of them probably have cake daily, in fact, and—"

"Well, let's agree to disagree, Frank. When was the last time *you* walked the streets? And besides, those folks ain't laid up in bed like you are, waiting to have a heart attack."

Ouch. That was not called for. Mean and nasty. I really wish I did have the ability to go out. And anyway, why did she buy the cake when she won't let me have any?

Never refused to purchase it, did she?

He thought back to the day before. Weren't those crumbs she'd wiped off her face?

Then she'd continue as if nothing had happened, "I think what you want is a nice sandwich. Tuna again? No mayo because it's bad for you. All that nasty cholesterol and fat. And don't dare say I don't look after you, Frankie. Oh, Frankie, Frankie, Frankie… what to do with you?"

He never *would* dare say she didn't look after him. But it was like receiving 'care' from a dictator, always acting as if his agreement was a foregone conclusion, always denying him whatever it was he really craved. He'd managed to be polite to the first nurse. But starting with the second, he'd started making comments here and there, just to get a rise out of her. Never worked though. Certainly, it had never worked on Samantha.

She was from some part of the south and had the grating accent to prove it, but he could never get a straight answer out of her as to which particular state she was from. Probably Mississippi. White people from Mississippi most likely got accused of being racist just as the default, so it made sense she wouldn't want to tell a Yankee.

Frank was personally of the mind that he didn't need a night nurse. Nor did he think Annabella needed to waste all her days sitting with him. But she disagreed—of course, she did—so, there he was. A skull fracture, not to mention complex spinal fractures, had left him in constant pain and bedbound, at least for a time since progress would be slow.

Well, sure he could get out of bed if *they* allowed him to. But *they* did not—the dictators.

But although he would never admit to it, he kind of understood their point of view. Blinding headaches struck without warning, and his balance was touch and go at best.

The symptoms went on forever and seemed to shift with the wind, even to a point where he'd started to bleed internally for no damn reason on a couple occasions.

But still. Having someone sitting next to him all the time was too exhausting. Especially when they treated him like a child.

Not being allowed to drive made sense, and was reasonable.

But being confined to the bed for the majority of his day was intolerable. He hadn't been paralyzed in the wreck but around him, everyone behaved as if he had been. And as if he didn't have a functioning brain inside his skull anymore.

Never in a million years did I think I'd outlive Bianca, he thought. *I was older than her, and everyone knows men are supposed to die first. That's just the way of it. Plus, I smoked for ten years before Bianca made me quit. Living without her has never been a thing I prepared for.*

But in his current state, in a way, he was glad that she had died in the wreck.

Because if she hadn't, she would be the one caring for him, wasting her golden years getting things for him, fixing his meals and checking his vitals. She'd probably even have the whole house retrofitted to accommodate someone who was a fall hazard. No matter how much he protested, no matter how much stone-faced Samantha tried to help her with her tasks, Bianca would have been devoting every second to him, which would rip his soul apart to have to watch.

Her—and him—being spared that indignity was the only thing that kept him from blowing his own head off. Well, that and Daniella taking the gun from his nightstand, absconding with it.

Yes, even that had happened. He'd seen her do it shortly after they'd brought him home from the hospital, knowing what his mindset must be. Plus, she'd never liked guns in the house.

She'd hit the roof when he'd first shown it to her a few years back.

She'd been a teenager then, so he'd thought it was important she know about it and, if needed, knew how to fire the thing too.

But maybe it had been wrong of him; she'd set off crying as if her world had fallen apart, and he'd never forgotten what she had said. And he never would manage to forget it either.

"I never imagined my own parents would become a part of America's problem!"

"What problem, honey?" Frank had asked, taken aback.

No verbal answer ever did come, but she'd stormed off, sending a mass flurry of YouTube videos of random guys in their bedrooms. The Second Amendment should be repealed, they insisted as if their old folks knew nothing at all. These young people, what did they know?

It was really something, having your daughter look at you like a monster because some stranger on the internet had said so. Frank had tried taking her phone away after that.

Tried to. Bianca protested. "That's hardly fair on her, love. She's entitled to develop views of her own, even if they aren't the same as yours."

"You mean the same views as *ours,*" he corrected. "Not just mine."

"How d'you even know what my views are on guns, Frank?" Bianca had asked.

Well, he'd just sat quietly, pondering after that. Was he the only one in this household to believe in the right to bear arms? Thankfully, Bianca spoke up again.

"Look, Frank. All her friends' parents have guns, Frankie. She'll grow out of it.

She didn't though, just stopped complaining about it. Specifically, the complaints stopped after there was a home invasion a few blocks over. Just because they were in the suburbs didn't mean they were safe. But lately, after the collision and its terrible aftermath, she'd taken the opportunity to keep Frank from himself. God only knew what she'd done with that gun.

Probably thrown it in the Long Island Sound. He didn't dare ask.

Annabella had witnessed Daniella taking the gun too, but she also didn't say anything. She probably approved, honestly. *She's such a good girl. Not that her sisters aren't. But Annabella always makes things easy.* Frank and Bianca were honestly spoiled by her, rather than the other way around. A supremely unfussy baby, who was hardly ever ill, had somehow miraculously grown into a toddler who ate her vegetables with gusto and accepted the word *no* on the first try.

Then, Viviana—their middle girl—had come along four years later, and both Bianca and Frank had to reorient their expectations. Oh, so it was true? Babies cried even when not hungry?

Did toddlers really throw things and intentionally bite their siblings? Good heavens!

They had genuinely believed such behavior to be a sign of poor parenting. It had been humbling, to say the least. "Oh, so now you have yourselves a real kid!" people would say.

And it was true. Not that young Annabella hadn't been real but now, they were discovering what it was that made other parents despair. A naughty child, a wayward and stubborn one.

Far later, and true to form, Annabella had been the one to step up in place of her mother after Mom was killed in the crash. Not just because she was the eldest either.

It was because she was single with no kids in school anymore; she just saw there was responsibility to be taken, and she would be the one to take it. Besides, she was able to work remotely, and her boss was very understanding, so of course it would have to be her.

Well, in all honesty, she hadn't been single, not technically, not back then.

But right now, she was, in every sense of the word.

In Frank's opinion, she'd been single for a while now. He'd seen it coming.

It was only just now that *she'd* realized it.

"Brad took me to dinner, and I thought *this is it,*" Annabella said, spreading her hands wide, the smile on her face belying the tears in her eyes. "He's finally going to propose. He's finally decided I'm not a blood-sucking hypergamous woman who's just after his wealth. But no…"

She sniffed and looked over at Frank. "Do you know what he said, Pop? That he felt like he wasn't the priority in my life anymore and that wasn't acceptable to him and wasn't the kind of life he wanted for himself. And—get this—he had better options than a thirty-five-year-old!"

That son of a bitch! There was a whole lot Frank had to say about Brad, but his daughter was hurting and she didn't need him rubbing salt in the wound with any *I told ya so's.*

So, he restricted himself to, "I'm sorry, honey."

Really, what else could he say?

In fact, he'd tried to warn her this clown wasn't serious from the beginning. That he'd take the best years of her life and leave her behind. She hadn't spoken to him for months after he'd said that to her, so he'd never criticized Brad again. But now, everything predicted had come true. He'd only ever wanted to keep her from ever feeling the pain she was experiencing now.

"He's acting as if I wasn't twenty-eight when we met! Like he didn't take all my fertile years. I got old together *with him!* And he acts like it's something I did *to* him."

"You're not old, honey. You still have time. Medicine's amazing now if you end up needing a bit of help to start a family. You just need to find a man who's serious from the get-go."

She gave a brief nod, looking up at the ceiling, exasperated. That wasn't new, of course.

But he couldn't stay quiet anymore.

It was one thing if Annabella was happy being single. Daniella certainly seemed to be. But Annabella wasn't. She wanted a husband, longing for children, craving to end up as one of those Italian grandmothers with a table full of descendants all raving about her cooking.

She was seeing that future slipping away and it broke Frank's heart to have to see it.

What could he do?

He was the one holding her back, no doubt about it. How could she devote time to meeting a good man who would value her when she was spending all of her time here? Brad was a goon and a selfish prick, but he had been right about one thing, that her time was spoken for. She wouldn't be able to make any man her priority with her feeble dad gumming up the works.

Her father's banged-up body was a prison for his daughters.

He had watched his girls sob over their mother and been helpless to make it better, unable to even go to the funeral as he'd still been in the hospital at the time. So, it had fallen on the girls to work with the church. They'd even had to go through his and Bianca's phones to contact all their friends because Frank hadn't even been able to speak well enough to help them with who to call.

In the end, it had been Muriel, Bianca's Jewish friend, who'd come through like a star, the one to coordinate with the women's groups at St. Francis of Assisi to make sure the repast was in order and that a visiting priest was brought in for the funeral Mass. Father Thomas had been in a car accident lately as well. Just a broken leg, but he was an old man, so they'd had to bring in a young guy from Rhode Island. Muriel was a saint, taking that burden off his girls.

If he ever got out of this bed, he'd do something nice for her.

God bless her.

Samantha came back into his room, her scrubs stretched to nearly the breaking point across her hips. Clearly, those were unisex scrubs, as if there could be such a thing.

As irritating as he found her sometimes, he had to hand it to her, she was always friendly with his girls. And they seemed to like her.

"Girl, did I hear you say that dog-ass Brad had the nerve to dump you?" Samantha asked, genuine anger in her voice. "I'ma tell you what I do. I put it right there in my profile. *I love God and I am looking to be a wife. And if you ain't looking for that, keep steppin'.*"

She sat down on the edge of Frank's bed, putting a consoling hand onto Annabella's arm. "Yeah, I get fewer messages, but the ones I do get, they're good options, girl, you see, cause I'm sayin' exactly what I want and will accept. And you know what I found…" She lowered her voice into a conspiratorial whisper. "The ones who ain't much to look at, sometimes they're the best ones when they come up to bat, you hear what I'm saying?"

Annabella laughed, a loud, long, genuine laugh. *God love you, Samantha.*

"You might be right. Once I start dating again, I'll keep that in mind."

Samantha patted her hand. "I know you got a lot on your mind right now. But it'll be all right."

Not as long as I'm here, making her feel miserable and guilty, and tying up her life for her, Frank thought bitterly, though he'd keep his negative musings to himself.

She had her whole life ahead of her. Or she should do.

She shouldn't be chained to his specially ordered hospital bed. She shouldn't be forced to be surrounded by her mother's things, not even able to get rid of them.

He'd told her multiple times it was okay to go through them. It was okay to give some to Bianca's friends. And to give the rest to charity. Or even to throw them away if it came to that; what was the sense in holding onto old things just for the sake of it?

Sentimental value, some said. But what was sentimental about a load of old tat and a bunch of clothes that would never be worn again? He didn't need them, did he? And his girls wouldn't be wearing those garments unless they came into fashion again soon, which was highly unlikely.

And honestly, looking at old clothes still hanging in the closet just made him want to die.

But after that discussion, Annabella had changed the subject every time he asked her about it. Her mom was gone, she accepted that. But it seemed to Frank that she couldn't move on as long as her dad was still there. Like she said, she couldn't put her personality onto it.

"You wouldn't really like me to get rid of Mom's things, would you, Pop? I know you say I should do it, that I should make this place more about me and less about you and Mom but… but it's got to be awfully upsetting for you. And I don't think I should, not while…"

Yeah, not while I'm still breathing. That's what you mean, isn't it?

He looked wearily at Samantha's back as she continued chatting with Annabella, the two of them happy in their girl talk. Should he ask Samantha to talk to his girls about Bianca's things? Would that help? Maybe they'd listen if *she* spoke to them.

Lord knew, they weren't inclined to listen to him.

CHAPTER 2

"I watched my dad pull the slide back on the gun, holding it to the rear so he could peer into the chamber. Any debris stuck in there could mean a jam at best, or a deadly backfire at worse."

Annabella turned the page of the book, looking up at Frank with a mischievous smile. "Remember Daniella swiping your firing pin that one time? You were so mad."

"I certainly do," he said, definitely not smiling. "She's lucky your mother stepped in because I was ready to ground that girl for the rest of high school. Although…" He trailed off, allowing the faintest hint of a smile to rise. "The fact that she was able to disassemble the pistol to find the firing pin says I did something right. Quite something, now I think about it."

Annabella nodded, returning to reading aloud. It wasn't a book he had ever heard of before, but it was popular, said

Annabella, all about a father—an old-school mobster—who'd drawn his daughter into a life of crime. She'd recommended he read it but hell no, he'd protested, at least initially. What kind of a man could put his daughter at risk that way?

And why would anyone half decent want to read about it? Then he thought about it.

Sadly, that kind of thing wasn't unheard of; he'd even known one or two kids from the neighborhood who'd gotten into that life, the ones who'd watched *Goodfellas* and *The Godfather* and thought it would be glamorous to become scumbags. No, the book didn't sound good.

Annabella started reading it to him, and soon, he was hooked. So much for not showing any interest in that sort of garbage, then. But anyway, thankfully, it turned out the father wasn't actively trying to get his daughter into crime. She'd put herself in harm's way by dating a schmo; her dad pulled strings with his criminal contacts to get her out of it. But then she had to pay a debt. So, it made sense. Still not great parenting, but you did the best you could, he believed.

Book one lay behind them now, and they were onto book two.

Frank was enjoying it, especially since Annabella was so good about going back and re-reading scenes if he fell asleep.

The second book was oddly both more enjoyable yet also a source of agitation. This was the one in which the daughter met a new guy, a criminal, but he treated her good.

Annabella's mouth got a little tight at those scenes. The voices she put on for each character slipped a little and in one spot, she even choked up a bit.

She suddenly looked up from the book at him, eyes wide; was she hoping to see her dad asleep so she could skip it? No. Well, in either case, she'd have seen he wasn't.

She continued reading.

Poor girl. Brad should count his lucky stars Frank wasn't cleared to drive. He'd surely have a few words for that lowlife if he was ever able to get his sorry lump of a body over to Queens.

It had been a couple days now since she'd told him about the breakup, but she'd refused to go into any deeper detail. He did ask though, the way a father usually wouldn't dare.

"Did you two ever talk about marriage early in the relationship, honey? Did he refuse to commit from the get-go, or did he just change his mind? Is he just flaky, or what?"

Annabella had pivoted at those questions. She'd never even begun answering, though it didn't seem as though she was avoidant, more that her mind had its priorities, meandering off.

"Well, Viviana came back to the apartment with me to get the rest of my stuff, Pop. It's kind of embarrassing how little of it is actually mine. All those years together and I didn't think anything of just becoming an extension of his life. Never carving out space of my own."

"That's only because you were committed, honey. It's really not a bad thing and don't let anyone tell you otherwise because they'd be wrong. He's bad for taking advantage of it. The thing is, when you meet the one, you just know it and you both put in the effort, and it's—"

There I go again. Being opinionated. Now, I've just told her that Brad didn't think she was anyone special. Better zip it, Frank. You're only going to make matters worse. Well done, Pop.

He'd tried to keep his tone soft, not wanting her to think he was judging her. Yet he *was* kind of judging her. The way girls these days just allowed guys to hang around and take up space. No commitment, no plan, no investment. So, what was the point? To have someone to go to the movies with? It was insane! Hadn't he been a good enough father that his girls knew their worth?

That they deserved to be treated like queens, not like trash to be used and discarded?

It was hard to deny that maybe he'd made some missteps, looking at his eldest and youngest. But Viviana at least had done it right. His sweet middle girl, the one who seemed to go out of her way to be invisible. Quiet, bookish, and entirely unbothered by people's opinions, Frank figured she would be the one to die as an old cat lady… and be thoroughly pleased with that outcome.

But no. After Viviana graduated high school, she'd gone to work at a bakery. No college for her. "Give the money you saved to Daniella," she'd said as if it was an afterthought. Then, once she turned twenty-five, she'd created her online dating profile which Frank wasn't crazy about to say the least, just a pretty picture of her and a few simple lines.

I'm Annabella, looking for a husband who'll be faithful and kind! In return, I'll be a wife who's faithful and kind. Also, I make really great pies.

That was it. No long list of dealbreakers or paragraphs about her idiosyncrasies, of which there were many. And less than a year later, she and Pavel got married.

A Polish boy, as you might have guessed, he was a mechanic specializing in commercial vehicles, holding a contract with the city to repair some of their garbage trucks. A hard worker and straight talker, he'd been weirdly enthusiastic about CS Lewis books, but Frank could see how Viviana would find that kind of specific hobby appealing. And they were happy, trying for a baby in fact, which was why of all three of his girls, Viviana was here the least often.

But Frank preferred that, glad she was looking to the future. Glad she was a devoted wife and proud of being one too, even taking classes on how to be the best mother. Even so, walking her down the aisle on her special day, Frank had been keen to ensure it was what she truly wanted, that she wasn't just doing what she believed he or society expected.

"All I've ever wanted was to be like Mom," she clarified shyly, keeping her voice down so no one but Frank could hear. "And all I ever want from now on is to be nearly as successful in love as you and Mom were." It had brought a knot into his throat, giving him a hard time composing himself before *Here Comes the Bride*.

Now, with Annabella just five years away from forty, the future she wanted for herself seemed to be slipping away. Older ladies wanting to carry babies usually had to pay for drugs and treatments, and God knew, that could get expensive, even if she found a good man to marry.

She'd be able to pay for it all so easily with your life insurance, Frank. And if she struck lucky on the first try, then she'd have all that money left over to help the kid grow up.

The thought came suddenly and fleetingly, creeping into his head entirely unbidden, quickening his heart and making the noisy machine next to him beep louder.

"Are you okay, Pop?" Annabella asked, her eyes going wide, putting the book down immediately and rushing to his side. He tried to avoid giving an exasperated look.

Now, she rested her hand against his forehead, anxious over his state of health as ever, then darting her eyes over to the EKG as if she had sole responsibility for whether he lived or died.

Her face seemed to say, *please don't say he's going into cardiac arrest again.* She was always frantic these days, always under stress, and it was all his fault. Figuratively speaking, it killed him to see her this way, his beloved girl living such a restricted life since his accident.

With a relieved sigh, she finally sat back down, but a deep worry crease remained between her eyes. That was painful to see too, only serving to emphasize her advancing years.

No one could help noticing that her skin was no longer fresh and dewy, and when she scowled, she maybe didn't even know it failed to bounce back these days. As ugly as it was to have to admit it, her skin often resembled a crumpled paper bag. Then there were all the pregnancy hormones to consider; what havoc might they wreak on a woman's body at her age?

No, if she was eager to get pregnant and have a family, it had better be soon.

For one thing, Frank didn't want his grandchild to be one of those who got bullied because his mom looked like a grandparent. Time was running out. And fast.

"Pop?" Annabella inquired again, resting a hand on his arm. "You never answered."

"I'm fine, honey. Keep going," he assured her, finally mustering a response to what it was she'd asked several minutes ago.

"All right, Pop," she said quietly. "I suppose you *are* doing fine, considering. But you look so—" She never did finish. Her bottom lip was wavering, voice cracking.

This was obviously all too much for her because she thought it was all too much *for him.* And he, in turn, worried for her. They were too entangled in each other's emotions, tormented by them. Her eyes lingered on his, as if seeking to read his hidden thoughts, and as if struggling.

"I really am fine, love," he said. "You need to think less about me, and more about yourself."

That statement seemed to send her reeling, and she'd plainly decided he'd had enough storytelling for one day; she put the book down.

"Pop, I'm going to run to my car for a jacket," she expressed, teary. "I'll be right back." She got up with a hop as if he were timing on her on how fast she could get to the car and back.

***

With a gasp long and guttural, his throat sore from the effort of it, Frank jolted into waking.

The room was dark and stiflingly hot. Where had Annabella gone? Ah. She had almost fled the room, hadn't she? Yet that had been long ago! Hours, surely.

Had she never returned, or was it the case that he'd dozed off? If the former, he was scared for her mental health. If the latter—that was horribly rude of him.

He looked over at the alarm clock, the bright blue numbers glowing back.

3:30 a.m.

When had he fallen asleep?

Muffled voices drifted into the room, but loud enough to hear. Magnum PI was on TV.

Samantha loved to watch old shows in the night. Nice as it was to see a young lady with good taste, in this one instance, he rather wished she were in his room when he needed her there.

But as ever, he was too prideful to call out and ask her to come. "Hey, Nurse Samantha! I've had a horrible dream. Can you come sit with me like a child until I fall asleep again?"

That absolutely would not be happening. So, Frank settled back down into bed, his sheets so damp he turned on the light and pushed the covers back. Had he peed himself?

No, just sweat.

He had escaped the indignity of having to wear a diaper too, at least for now.

But even that was coming. Slowly but surely, his vitals were getting a little bit worse, his mobility just a little less, and the looks on his daughters' faces more than a little less hopeful.

In his dream, he'd been sitting in Daniella's room, right beside her bed. But there were two other beds as well, three laid out side by side, all three of his girls lying there. Only they were old and alone, and wholly unable to move or speak. He'd wandered confused from bed to bed, trying to wake them, looking for someone to help him, but there was no one. Only himself.

He didn't have to be a board-certified psychiatrist to know what the dream meant. The last thing he wanted was for the girls to have to waste their best years on him. Annabella deserved better. And even though Daniella didn't come around a lot for now, she loved her sister too much to let her bear the burden alone for too long. She would start to take an active role in his care as well, flushing away her own future prospects too. And so would Viviana.

She would probably take her eventual kids with her to check on Grandpa, instead of taking them to fun and enriching activities. Those poor kids would have to endure sitting at the bedside and he could just envisage them saying, "Aww, do we have to come? It's booooring!"

The thought of it all only made him sicker than he was.

When they had been little, his girls had always been better off with him around, his presence helping them grow up to be intelligent and moral young women. But now… that wasn't the case.

Now, his presence could only hurt them, and it was all set to get even worse.

He couldn't allow it. He wouldn't.

CHAPTER 3

Like all good Southern women, Samantha had a tendency to say, 'Oh, bless your heart' when someone asked her something and she didn't want to be rude in her response.

Or if she thought someone was being stupid but didn't want to actually call it out.

Frank knew this about her because the woman had every phone conversation on speaker, regardless of whether she was in the living room or in his bedroom. Why? Why did she do this? Why did today's young women *always* do this? Were they so proud of everything they had to say? He could not see why, if so. The upside of her particularly irritating habit was that he was starting to get a good handle on her passive aggressiveness.

He'd been there when Samantha's mother asked if she was coming home for Christmas for once. *Oh, bless your heart but I can't; the holidays are so busy at work.*

When some guy—a boyfriend possibly—called her up to ask who the actor from Breaking Bad was: *Oh, bless your heart, you know who that is.*

They had another way of doing things down south.

If some schmo had called up Frank because he didn't know who Bryan Cranston was, Frank would have just called him a dipshit, making him guess until the idiot remembered. Or until he Googled it, exactly what he should have done in the first place instead of calling Frank.

Whenever Samantha said *bless your heart* to someone, it always came with a very particular facial expression. Eyebrows up, rapid blinking, and mouth pinched up in a bad impression of a smile. And he had recently noticed something; it was that she often gave Frank that same face whenever he asked her to please not do his stretching exercises today or if she could please not turn down the AC at night. Never a response, just that *bless your heart* smile.

It made him want to punch her sometimes.

But not really, because she was a nice girl. And a good nurse.

But her passive aggressive habits had apparently started to rub off on Annabella too.

That morning, he'd given her a moment to settle in—and to make sure Samantha had gone—before sitting up in bed and asking, "I'd like to talk to you about something if I may?"

It was something important and he hoped she would hear it in his tone.

She'd sat down across from him, crossing her legs, setting the book in her lap, then silently waited for him to say what he had to say.

"Honey, I know this last year hasn't been easy for you. I know you've had to bear the brunt of everything with your mother passing and with me not be a hundred percent."

He licked his lips, almost embarrassed to have made that whopping understatement. He continued, "But I've been thinking that it's time I moved on. To be with your mother. And I wonder if maybe you'd help me… help me to do that."

He had more to say, but as he took a breath to continue on with his request and make it more specific, Annabella was looking down at the hardcover book in her lap, picking at the cellophane cover, her signature nervous tic. Anytime she got in trouble, or if he and Bianca had to give the girls bad news, Annabella would always drop her head and fidget with whatever she had at hand.

Frank didn't continue. What would have been the point? Sometimes, something would be troubling her deeply, and he'd noticed that it could take her a long time to reply if at all.

Sometimes, she left the unthinkable things unthought, and the unspeakable ones unsaid. Maybe this was one such time. Possibly. Who really knew?

He just kept looking at her, waiting for her to talk when she was ready.

If ever.

After a while, she stopped picking at the book cover, instead smoothing it with the palm of her hand as if in some sort of apology to it, the way you might stroke a kitten after accidentally standing on its tail. Then with a deep breath, she shifted her face into the *bless your heart* face, then looked down and opened the book in her lap. The words came, but not meaningful ones.

Not the ones Frank had been hoping to hear. Ones about death, about slipping away into the next world. About leaving his precious girls unburdened and free to continue their own lives.

She spoke simply. "It's a funny thing about doing business with crooks. Sometimes, they have more honor than the cops and the lawyers ever could."

Frank let out a short, outraged laugh. One she purposefully ignored and kept right on reading.

He'd expected her to refuse his request, of course. Maybe she'd even stomp out of the room. But he'd been okay with needing to bring it up multiple times to make her understand. He had his whole case laid out to explain it to her. If need be, he would ask again and again. Until…

He would be out of pain, he'd say. She and her sisters would be financially set. If they chose to sell his house, that would be another injection of cash. All three could move on with their lives, just as he wanted. Not out of fear or dementia. Not even out of depression. It was just the right thing to do. He had it all ready to explain to her. She only needed her to be willing to hear.

But he hadn't expected this. There had never been a time any of his girls had completely ignored him. It certainly wasn't something he would have expected from her. Daniella could always be counted on for a sassy retort, but never the silent treatment.

He sat there for a moment, seething at the disrespect. Yeah, that's what it was. No other word for it really. *Disrespect*. Did they view him as so helpless and feeble he didn't even have the right to express his wishes anymore? He was just a stupid, pathetic old man they wouldn't listen to? A burden? Was that what he had already become in their eyes?

But then, he saw Annabella swallow hard between paragraphs, her voice wavering as she read aloud. She was fighting back tears, refusing to look up at him. No, she did not view him as a stupid old man. She saw him as her father, and she was afraid of what was to come.

He sighed, mostly in disgust at himself, then adjusted his pillows so he could recline comfortably. *It was wrong of me to even ask. Asking for her help will only add to her burden... not take it away, like I want to. And now, look what I've done. I've upset her.*

He stared up at the ceiling, which still had the old-fashioned popcorn texture, silently kicking himself for being a son of a bitch to his favorite daughter. No, parents weren't supposed to have favorites, but they all did. And Annabella was his, which was why she'd been the one he wanted to ask in the first place. But that was wrong. He saw that now.

It was all too soon for her after losing her mother. Now, he was suggesting he'd rather be wherever Mom was, and not here with his girls. He was stupid and thoughtless.

Obviously, she wasn't ready to even contemplate losing him too. Hell, even if he passed peacefully in his sleep, she would probably view that as a personal failure.

That was probably why she wouldn't even get rid of her mother's clothes. If she just did everything perfectly, then it would turn out all right, wouldn't it?

She had been like that since she was a girl, full of weird little rituals and an almost unsettling determination to 'do the right thing' as if that would somehow bring order to the world around her. Well, now he had to repair the damage. He should have known she wouldn't be ready to tell him goodbye, that she couldn't accept that loss too. Not on her watch.

It was selfish of him to even entertain such thoughts, callous, self-serving and cruel. Yet even now, all he wanted was to be with Bianca again. She was the one who had explained Annabella's quirks to him. She was the one who could see beyond the habits and right into the reasoning. If things had been different, she'd have made a hell of a psychiatrist. Or a nun.

Frank had never shied from admitting he'd never been a perfect Catholic. Maybe not even a mildly good one. But he had been raised in the Church, and he quite liked being Catholic.

Liked the Mass and the formality of it all, liked having priests and the solemn nature of everything. But as for the doctrine… that was something else.

For instance, he never believed for one second that the host turned into the literal body of Christ, something all good Catholics were supposed to buy into, but how could he? That was a wackadoo idea if ever he'd heard one and it wasn't even introduced until late in the Church's history. What were they all supposed to be then, cannibals? As far as he was concerned, that was never supposed to be taken literally, not even when Jesus had said it to the apostles.

But saying that kind of thing aloud wasn't really something he made a habit of doing. Bianca's face had turned solid white to hear him ask her if she believed in transubstantiation.

"Frank, you sound like a Protestant," she'd scolded him.

And maybe he was, in his beliefs anyway. But there was no way he was going to one of those glorified rock concerts the Protestants called church either!

And he most definitely wasn't bringing his girls there.

Then, he'd heard all about the so-called youth pastors. People made a lot of jokes about pedophile priests but for some reason, they had nothing to say when it came to goateed men in their twenties taking advantage of young girls in 'youth group'.

No, having his family go to two different churches wasn't something Frank was interested in. And Bianca definitely wasn't either. Besides, he figured it was okay to still go to a church even if some of the dogma rubbed you wrong. He agreed on the big stuff, like the afterlife.

That was what mattered, wasn't it?

There was a heaven, and there was a hell. That much he knew.

But again, he got hung up on what the Bible said, rather than the Vatican. And the Bible was actually pretty vague on what it was exactly that would get you to hell. Idolatry for certain. But after that, it seemed to get muddier, at least from his perspective.

And now, here he was, a Catholic, thinking about—no, not 'thinking about', rather contemplating—suicide. The Catechism said suicide was the only unforgiveable sin, that it would send you straight to hell with no exceptions. But in his younger years, he'd tried to find that for himself in the Bible. He couldn't spot it.

Not that he'd been considering the notion of suicide back then but a friend of Bianca's had actually offed herself upon finding out her husband was cheating on her.

Well, maybe not a friend. More of an acquaintance because Frank had never even met the lady. Cheryl was her name. And Bianca had been lighting a candle every day for her since, praying for her lost friend to be spared damnation.

He wanted to help Bianca feel better, so he'd had a chat with his priest.

Father Paul—a Vietnamese fellow, oddly enough—had been in charge of the parish then, and he'd been happy to take Frank's questions.

What about Marines who threw themselves on top of grenades to save the other men in the fox hole? Or the bodyguard who'd take a bullet for the politician employing him? Did that mean they were going to hell? Had they committed an unforgiveable sin? And didn't Jesus himself say "Greater love hath no man than this, that a man lay down his life for his friends?"

Father Paul had been a good sport and turned out to be a surprisingly well-read theologian, which wasn't always the case with parish priests.

He explained that it wasn't the act of ending one's life that was the unforgivable sin.

It was the associated despair; the blasphemy lay in believing yourself to be irredeemable. That was Judas's sin, not actually the act of hanging himself.

Christ redeemed all, you see, small sinners and big ones, even the ones who cursed His name so it was a grievous insult to decide life was not worth living because it couldn't be redeemed.

It was a satisfying answer, one he took back to Bianca in triumph. Her friend might not be in hell after all. Just maybe purgatory for intentionally punishing her husband for his infidelity.

And thankfully, it *had* made her feel a bit better.

Now all these years later, Frank knew he wasn't in despair either; he had not actually given up on life, more that it had given up on him, rendering him a dreadful burden to his next of kin. Would it not, therefore, be a noble and gracious gesture to step down in such a circumstance?

And he certainly wasn't under the misbegotten belief that his problems were beyond the reach of God's mercy. He just understood what God intended for him, that God had made His mind up where old Frank was concerned and just wanted to speed it up.

Frank was dying. Slowly, painfully, and in an exceptionally expensive manner.

He wasn't looking to die to stop his own suffering.

It was to stop his girls from suffering. The grief they would feel at his passing would be far less damaging and soul destroying than spending day after day in this room, wondering when it would happen, depleting his bank account and theirs just to give him a few more months.

That was not what a good father did. Just like the cop or the soldier, he was willing to give his life to save others. So, hell couldn't be on the cards for him. If purgatory were a real thing which, again he had his doubts about, but if it happened to be, maybe he'd end up there.

But not for sparing his girls.

He'd go to purgatory for the times he'd snapped at Bianca when he'd been in a bad mood. Or maybe for the time

Viviana had asked him to pick her up after school because she had a Drama Club meeting… and he hadn't shown up.

He'd gone out for a beer instead, remembering far too late he had somewhere to be. But even that was unintentional, so maybe he'd be spared purgatory. In any case, could it be worse than this? Could it be worse than languishing in a sweaty bed, unable to look after himself?

Sure, his many offenses, he could see needing to burn them all off before being allowed into heaven and he was willing to inject the effort.

He wasn't a perfect man and definitely hadn't been a perfect husband. He could admit he might need some cleansing before seeing Bianca again in the afterlife.

Annabella's voice had stopped shaking by now. She had started doing the voices again, which he liked. He smiled at her. And in this moment, it grew clear; he wouldn't bring it up to her again. He wouldn't try to convince the other two either. Hell, assisted suicide was still illegal in New York, and he was asking his girl to get involved? What was he thinking?

Maybe he was losing his faculties as well as his mobility. But then again, *why* would it be illegal? He wracked his memory for any news report; might a law have been passed, some sort of regulation making it easier, less punishable? No, nothing came to mind, and he watched the news more than most people since there wasn't much else to do from the goddamn bed.

Even if it would just be a fine that his girl might get for assisting his passage, he wouldn't let that fall on her. It was bad enough to admit he couldn't take them all out to eat or go walking in the park together like they used to. He certainly wasn't going to get them in trouble with the law.

Getting rid of himself—*by* himself—was the best, most loving thing he could do.

And that was exactly how it would be.

CHAPTER 4

"Just out of curiosity, Samantha," Frank planned on asking. "What exactly would happen if I stopped taking my pills? I mean all of them? All at once? I feel as if I might be getting addicted, and that's a bad thing, especially for someone in my condition."

It was a feeble and nonsensical excuse. But it was all he had. And already, he knew she would see right through it, and he could already imagine her shrill tones inside his head.

"Now, I never did hear such a load of nonsense! You're very sick, Frank! Getting addicted to lifesaving medications is the least of your worries, believe me! I never heard anything so ridiculous in all my days. Addiction, indeed. Now here, take these, they'll calm you down."

And with that, she would thrust another clutch of pills at him.

What she couldn't know was that he already hadn't swallowed the pills Samantha had given him last night. These were the ones for nerve pain, which were different than the regular painkillers. He hadn't noticed any side effects from missing a dose. Far from it, actually.

He felt oddly better today, more alive, more vital.

But he knew enough about medicine to know stopping any serious drugs suddenly could do bad things. Googling had dredged up a bunch of sites that said:

Maybe it'll be fine.

Or maybe you'll die a terrible vomiting death.

Maybe you won't notice any difference or even start to feel better.

Or maybe your heart will fail, leaving you kicking and writhing in agony on the floor, wracked by silent screams. Consult your doctor before reducing or stopping any medications.

Thank you, Internet. Very helpful.

He would have to give Samantha a try. Today, she was wearing a cranberry-colored set of scrubs that fit her perfectly. No awkward stretching across her backside or chest, even though both of which were far larger than those of any woman in his family.

The scrubs had the back profile of a seated cat sewn on the chest and he could tell they were several years old. Didn't he remember her complaining to Annabella that the company didn't make them anymore? But she would 'hold onto these until they fell apart.' Good for her; they looked nice, though he hoped not to be around when her voluminous shape burst the seams.

As usual, Samantha was being her same standoffish self, declining to answer his question about what would happen if he withdrew from all the drugs. No; she was keeping her views quiet. She was always happy to help flip him over in bed. Happy to steady him while he stretched. And always happy to dope him up.

But she wasn't interested in one stitch of insightful conversation on this topic. "Why you askin' me that?" she snapped. "You feelin' all right today, Mister Vitale? You thinkin' 'bout stoppin' them drugs because you're going to spring right outta that bed? Don't tell me the Lord has dropped by and healed you?"

She cast him the sort of look a teacher would give a naughty student.

"Yeah, something like that. I feel fine. Just fine."

Obviously, he'd have to find out about withdrawals and side effects the hard way. He'd give it a few days, see how he felt. His other pills were opioids, so he could expect more withdrawals from those than from the ones for the nerve pain, which were anticonvulsants. He'd stick his dose tonight under his mattress with the others. They were hard tablets, not gel tabs, so he didn't have to worry about anything dissolving and spilling out onto the floor or making a hellish stain.

That would be hard to explain. He could just envisage the apoplectic rage on Samantha's face as the frothy white powder came oozing from between his mattress and box spring.

"Now what in tarnation is this, Mister Vitale?"

The thought made him chuckle, and at least that extracted a grudging half-smile out of Samantha as she read whatever was on her phone.

***

Hours later, Frank lay back, pretending to be asleep, Samantha's signal to give him one final check before retreating to the living room to watch her shows for the rest of the night. Like clockwork, she did exactly that, checking his vitals, straightening his covers, and gently grazing her thumb across his cheek. Yeah, Samantha was a good girl like that.

Once she was gone, Frank reached over, quietly opening the nightstand drawer. He didn't turn on the lamp; Samantha would see that from the living room, and it also took an agonizingly long time to open the drawer without any squeaks or creaks.

Soon, the tinny sound of machine gun fire was coming from the television, and he sighed in relief, pulling his laptop from the drawer with no more need for stealth.

Frank loved things or loathed things, scarcely ever in between about anything,

And one thing he loathed was email.

Email was a vile innovation, only for people you didn't care about, such as coworkers or a pushy makeup saleslady who insisted on leaving free samples on the doorstep a few times a year. But in this case, he would have to use email to contact Marty, his estate lawyer.

He owed Marty a few lines at least.

Ideally, he would call him during the day to talk to him, but he couldn't risk Annabella overhearing. But he didn't want Marty to think something was wrong either, or that Frank was mad at him for some reason, avoiding him.

So, he made a point to write a longer email than he otherwise would have.

Hi Dave,

It's Frank Vitale. I'm sorry I haven't been in touch lately. I hear you've been speaking with

Annabella, so you know I've been out of commission here for a bit.

She tells me your office sent a flower arrangement for Bianca's service, and I want you to

know that means a lot to me. I'm sure Annabella must have sent you a thank-you card too

because that's just how she is.

But we are truly grateful that you have been thinking of us during this time.

Given my health, I'm sure you understand that I want to have my own affairs in order. When

Bianca passed, we hadn't updated our paperwork in a long time. That turned out okay since

our family hadn't changed since we originally wrote it up. But if I kick off, I want to make

sure my girls and any future children they have are in a good place.

With that in mind, I've attached a list of updates to my will and healthcare directive. Can you

make sure you make those changes into new documents? If it's not too much trouble, I'll also

have to have you send a notary sent here instead of coming to your office.

The doctor still won't let me drive and I don't want to trouble the girls. They all have me wrapped up in cotton wool for some reason.

Anyway, I appreciate you helping me wrap up these loose ends.

Thanks,

Frank V.

He pushed send, smiling at the memory of the way email used to be. In the nineties, every time you sent an email, it was a big event with a loud whooshing sound and then a ding, almost as if the computer was congratulating you on figuring out how to do it. Luckily for him, computers didn't do that anymore as the TV in the living room had gone much quieter now.

It had been an oversight on Frank's part, going so long without updating the will. If he had died right alongside Bianca, that scumbag Brad would have ended up with a cash payment.

Frank had left him some money too as it never occurred to him that he and Annabella wouldn't eventually get married. That may be the only blessing of him lasting a bit longer.

He'd be able to get the paperwork in order. Tie up the loose ends, dot the i's and cross the t's.

"Paperwork is important, Frankie," his father had always told him. "It's not just for Wall Street types. A working man needs to have all his papers in order too. In fact, for the likes of us, it's more important because the ones we leave behind may struggle, you see?"

In truth, Frank's father hadn't possessed a whole lot of good life lessons to give him. But it turned out he'd been right about the paperwork thing.

Paul Vitale—pronounced Vy-Tal when he'd gone looking for work—had been your average New York factory worker. The son of an Italian immigrant, he had always been a hard worker; he was also a good Catholic, living a respectable life. It was hard to say much else about him.

Frank's dad hadn't had much of an exciting life; he'd gone to work, and then after work, he'd always go 'out,' something his mother never questioned, only scolding the young and curious Frank if he had the nerve to. And whenever Frank's father had been at home, it was as though he wasn't anyway since he'd usually be asleep. And at one point, just like a lot of men of his generation, Paul Vitale had gone to war, in the Pacific region.

But that was really all Frank knew.

He had never been allowed to talk or ask about the war either. Or about anything really. In those days, children were seen and not heard—and ideally, they wouldn't be seen much either.

It was a lonely life.

Frank had once asked his mother why he was an only child when all his friends had so many siblings. Well, the answer to that impertinent question was that she'd slapped him so hard his lip swelled. Looking back, Frank thought maybe the old man had trouble in the bedroom.

Maybe he couldn't perform. Or maybe he was just shooting blanks.

Either way, you didn't talk about things like that back then as his mother's response showed.

Especially if you lived in Bensonhurst. Every man there was the king of his own world, one that started and ended at his own doorstep. No one had a right to ask anything.

A lot of married couples bickered, of course, as true then as it was now. Nothing wrong with it. But Frank's parents seemed to genuinely hate each other. Dad was out of the house more often than not, though he somehow managed to accrue plenty of wise-ass comments for his wife when he was home. And as for Frank's mom, sometimes when Dad would leave in the morning, she would audibly sigh in relief and sink onto the sofa, putting her feet up and lighting a cigarette.

Given that family dynamic, Frank was surprised how seriously his dad had taken his estate planning—the money he'd secretly saved to be handed out upon his death.

That was in addition to his life insurance policies. Yes, multiple policies.

New York was notorious for its bureaucracy, the way they made everything impossible. But Dad had every t crossed. And Mom was the most comfortable widow in Brooklyn. Frank had been ready to help her however she needed after Dad died of a heart attack at fifty-six. But she didn't need it. Maybe it was an apology for him being a mean ass while he was alive. Or maybe it was just in line with the way he thought things should be.

Paul was an old-school Italian American and made no apology for it. As far as he was concerned, a man put food on the table and fixed anything in the house that broke, and he had to skill up to be able to do it, taking his role seriously. A man was no use if he couldn't fix things.

A woman was to take care of the children and do as she was told. Children obeyed their parents and would get a job to support the household as soon as they were able.

And the man needed to make sure his wife was taken care of after he died.

That was the order of things and Paul Vitale had lived it to the letter.

Now that Frank thought about it, Viviana had a lot in common with her grandfather.

But thank God she wasn't as big of an asshole.

Frank put his laptop away and scrunched down in bed, moaning softly as he pulled the covers back up to his chest. If he knew anything about Marty, there would be a new will and medical directive waiting for him when he woke up. Then he would be ready.

He too would make sure his family was taken care of after he was gone.

CHAPTER 5

As expected, Marty got back to Frank in rapid fashion, with completed documents ready to be signed. As requested, he also took the liberty of sending over a notary to make everything official. Though the notary had been told to come after five, Annabella would be gone. Everything on the paperwork front was exactly as it should be. He'd be official.

The only question remaining was exactly how Frank was going to excuse himself from the party but he believed the pill stash under his mattress served as a terrific way out. The only concern on that front was if Samantha would get in trouble for it. He'd done some more searching on the internet, discovering that assisted suicide was only legal in ten states, plus Washington, DC. But not yet in New York, at least not for his specific circumstance.

And even where it was legal, there were pretty specific requirements.

None of which involved choking down a bunch of oxycontin.

There was also the snag in his life insurance, something he hadn't thought of right away. There would still be a payout if his death were ruled a suicide as he'd had the policy for decades; he had more than donated to the payout proceeds over the years.

But the payout would be reduced in the case of suicide, by about seventy percent.

That was no good. His girls would still clean up nicely with the rest of his assets, but he didn't want them to miss out on even one penny they were owed.

It was a shame he didn't live in Zurich. Apparently, they had a luxury *we'll help you die spa* right there for anyone to use. He'd never been to Switzerland before, which genuinely bothered him. If ever he got to travel internationally, Switzerland would be where he wanted to go.

Even more than Italy. He'd seen pictures, of course.

And more recently, there'd been all those videos on YouTube of people's experiences traveling there for the first time, amazed at the cleanliness of everything.

The YouTube people probably hailed from the Midwest, also taking note of the fact that though the Swiss were friendly, they didn't smile at you as you walked by them in the street. They didn't smile at you in New York either and it seemed to Frank that was the right approach. Why did people in the south and Midwest smile at you just for passing by?

It was all a touch weird.

But that was probably his Brooklyn upbringing.

It was not that he didn't have the money to travel overseas, just that Bianca didn't like flying. At all. She'd only ever been on a plane one time and even that was a trial.

While boarding, Frank had actually been optimistic, imagining he would coach her through it, explaining why the plane made those sounds or why there were bumps or vibrations. And she would feel better, and it all would be okay after that, and this would herald the start of new and exciting trips together! At last, they could take vacations farther away than the Jersey Shore.

But it *wasn't* okay. Bianca was so afraid the whole flight, so much so that a nice stewardess came along, eventually showing up back at the seats with a paper bag to breathe into.

"It's all right, ma'am. You see me walking around, right? If there was any danger, or if we were in for a bumpy ride, you'd see me right at the front strapped into my seat."

The lady had been pretty, even though she was older, maybe in her forties. Between him and the friendly stewardess, they'd been able to calm Bianca down enough that the pilot didn't need to call in a medical emergency. But Bianca had had enough, and besides, they couldn't rely on the same level of attention from cabin crew on every future flight. So, on the way back from her brother's wedding in Florida, they had rented a nice car and made the two-day drive.

So yeah, no going to Switzerland for Frank's final call.

No beautiful mountains, no crisp, clean air. No luxury suicide spas.

He had to wonder exactly what a 'luxury' death spa entailed anyway.

Did they give you one of those facial scrubs while administering the drug overdose? Or maybe you had a three-day package. Days one and two would be dedicated to pampering you, day three centering around seeing you off.

It gave him a chuckle to think about all those ladies in bath robes, green masks and cucumber slices stuck to their faces, all while someone stuck an IV full of a lethal drug into them.

Maybe he was being dismissive. By calling it a spa, it seemed like a business model targeted at women, an odd concept, surely. Was the wish to die more common in women?

Maybe Frank was biased, but he had a hard time believing that.

He only knew about the Swiss 'we'll kill you real good' spa after two American sisters made the news for going there to die. Funny thing was they were young and not terminally ill. So, of course, that prompted an investigation stateside. Was there any manipulation or foul play involved, they wanted to ascertain? Fair enough, Frank supposed. But technically, he wasn't terminally ill either. Despite that, shouldn't he be allowed to die on his terms and without his children—or his nurse—having to go through any hassle about it afterwards?

Frank stared out the window, straining to listen to the TV. Dear Samantha was still engrossed in her episode of Braveheart, and who could blame her? It was one of his favorites too.

This had been a good day. Since it was Friday, both Daniella and Viviana had come over today, giving Annabella the break that she undoubtedly needed. They'd played cards, Uno specifically, the girls using his blankets as the middle spot to slap their cards down.

It was fun, even though he couldn't help but notice Daniella had a new haircut. Half a haircut actually. She'd shaved one side of her beautiful hair off, leaving the other side long.

No matter how exciting the card game, he couldn't stop his eyes shiftily meandering back to that hair. Or the lack of it. The spot where it used to be.

Frank knew better than to make even one comment about Daniella's appearance; it was not allowed, a topic that would set a bad mood for the rest of the day. So he said nothing. Lucky for him, however, Viviana never cared about ruffling feathers. She had her eyes on it too, and nothing could stop her asking about it straight away.

"Is this your way of coming out as gay?" she asked, shuffling the Uno cards, and flicking them out to all three of them with practiced ease.

"Seriously, Viv, you don't have to be gay to get a side shave. That's *so* ignorant."

"Well, actually, you kinda do; everyone knows that. Even Dad. Don't you, Pop? Honestly, it's like wearing a massive billboard saying, *I'm a raving lesbian, come get me!* Or are you gonna be one of those straight girls who call themselves 'queer' so you can pretend to be gay without actually going down to kitty town?"

"Oh, my God!" Daniella shrieked in mock outrage, her face red.

She eyed Frank. This was evidently *so* not a subject for a man of his age. Or for a father, not in Daniella's eyes anyhow. But Viviana was almost collapsed in tears of laughter.

"Have to start calling you Kitty, do we?" she went on.

Frank covered his face with the blanket and laughed, trying to stifle it as best as he could, since laughing had the tendency to send his heartbeat off kilter. Coughing too. Or sneezing. Or getting up too fast. It seemed everything these days caused him arrhythmia. But worst luck, it never went all the way, never caused a heart attack. Well, damn that heart. It was too good.

It was actually good to hear his girls bicker. They were nine years apart, so had never really got that close sister bond that would have come from being children together.

Daniella hadn't been planned, something that seemed to bother her. But both he and Bianca had been overjoyed to find out another baby was on the way… once they got over the shock, of course. Bianca had been thirty-eight at the time she had Daniella, something he reminded Annabella of every now and again.

"Your mother was older than you and she got pregnant without even trying. Don't worry about it just yet, honey. It'll be in the genes that you'll have your own baby. And the one thing that kills fertility is stress, don't you know… So, ease up, and you'll be fine."

Viviana had once been there when he'd said it, and she'd cast her *but remember you also need to get laid* face. Didn't go down too well. It was true though. Would she need donor sperm?

Anyway, Frank's kindly comments didn't seem to cheer her up, so he laid off.

Today, it had been nice to have a day of just regular socializing.

The girls had chatted about their lives as always, kidding him too about his age.

"Hey Pop, I'm going to the Naval Museum when I go to DC next month. They've got a whole exhibit on Morse code. That was from your era, right?"

He'd just smiled and shaken his head. Did she have any idea how old Morse code was?

Her grandpa had used it in World War II but it had long since been declassified by the time Frank was old enough to join the military. Not that he did join of course… but if he had, there wouldn't have been any Morse code.

It was well after dark when Daniella and Viviana left, each giving him a kiss before leaving. Daniella lingered a bit longer to whisper in his ear, "If I did happen to be gay, like, just hypothetically, that would be okay with you, right, Pop?"

"So long as the girl treats you good, honey," he whispered back, smiling at her so she knew he meant it. He might have had a different answer under different circumstances. Hell, who was he kidding? He *definitely* would have had a different answer. If she'd asked before the accident, he probably would have said something about going through a phase and that she was just exposed to the wrong kind of men. From what he'd seen on the news, the college experience had really gone downhill these last few years. But there was no reason to say all that now.

He wanted her to be happy with someone who treated her like a princess. That was all.

Now alone in his room, he watched as the sun went down and the city lights came on, blindingly bright even all that way across the Sound. He couldn't see the ferry from here. It was too far. But he could see the Sound and the light glinting off the water, utterly beautiful.

All the bedrooms were on the second story and all had a great view, especially the master bedroom. Long Island wasn't as brightly lit as Manhattan obviously, but every part of New York was pretty well lit, no matter what time it was. How long had it been since he'd even gone into the city? It had never seemed worth the bother but still, it was odd to live somewhere and never see it. But everything he had known as a kid was gone now.

Well, a lot of the buildings were still there, but the neighborhoods had changed. The people had changed. He'd moved to the suburbs for a reason.

His father may have lived and died in Brooklyn, but Frank didn't have any desire to, especially after he and Bianca had been ready to start a family. He wanted an actual house, not some cramped apartment. And he wanted a yard too, a yard for a dog, something he'd always wanted. But Bianca turned out to be allergic, so that idea was scrapped. So, no flying for him, and no pooch either—but still, he had loved Bianca so much, he wouldn't much care.

No big deal as he'd said to her.

Anyway, most of his neighbors had dogs and no one minded if he came over to give them a pat on the head. He was just careful to wash his hands afterwards and sometimes, even needed to change his clothes as soon as he came home if the animal had jumped all over him.

Looking out at the Sound, the perfect idea came now.

It was the one that could solve everything. Why not go out one last time? See all the parts of the city that he'd walked as a kid, everything that had made him who he was. And he could see who lived there now, who was making memories in his old stomping ground.

There must have been a thousand dangers in the city for a sick, mobility impaired man. He knew for a fact there were.

That nice actor from *Honey, I Shrunk the Kids* had got mugged in broad daylight not long ago. In Central Park West, of all places! That meant no place in the city was truly safe, and that was exactly what Frank needed right now. He could go out with a flourish, have one last adventure, and let fate decide how the lights went out. For sure, if someone holed themselves up in a safe apartment, nothing bad could happen, right?

There could be a fire and that was about all, but he wouldn't hope for that; burning to death was not the best way to go. Anything but that.

No matter what the city served up to him, his girls would get everything they were owed and then some. And maybe they would even be happy for him, that he'd got up out of this bed one last time and taken his last breath in the same place he'd taken his first.

Yeah, that would be the way of it.

Smiling and with a deep sigh of contentment, Frank got fully under his covers and fell into the deepest, most satisfying sleep he'd had in a long time.

CHAPTER 6

Frank gave himself one week. One week to make sure all his loose ends were tied up and he had an opportunity to slip out. He had sent another email to Marty just to verify that his new paperwork was legal and binding, which it was. The next thing to sort out was an exit strategy. As it stood, there was no gap between Annabella leaving in the evening and Samantha arriving. Even if there were, if Samantha arrived and found him missing, she'd probably call out the National Guard. Or worse, she'd have the news issue one of those 'silver alerts' about him and then he really would have to kill himself immediately out of shame.

'Police have asked the public to be on the lookout for this demented old man who can't be trusted to move about freely. Please call 311 if you see him.' No thank you.

But this coming Friday would be different.

Annabella had an on-site work requirement, so she'd already asked Samantha to work a double that day, to which she had agreed.

But Frank couldn't help but notice she didn't look happy.

So, he did the only rational thing. He lied.

"Hey Samantha, how would you like this coming Friday off? For both shifts?" he asked, giving her his most disarming smile.

Holding one of his legs above the bed and rotating his ankle, she gave him an interested look. *Guess that's the best I'll get out of her.*

"Viviana and Daniella are coming up again, this time for the whole weekend. So, I'll have company the whole time, even with Annabella being out. I don't even need you here Friday night. I understand if you need the overtime, but I thought maybe you'd enjoy a date night."

Unexpectedly, Samantha beamed at him, her cheeks going a little pink.

Ah, so you found yourself a young man? I thought so!

Having found his ace in the hole, Frank now had a clear plan in place. All he had to do was keep Samantha occupied as much as possible if she tried to talk to Annabella at all.

The last thing he needed was her thanking his daughter for the time off. He could just imagine the angry stare Annabella would give him.

Between the two of them, they barely let him out of bed, let alone outside the apartment.

And he needed out of this apartment. Thinking about it now, even if he had a clean way to do it in which no one would be blamed, he wouldn't do it here. It wasn't fair to whoever found him. And definitely not fair to whoever had to clean up the mess.

It was just a matter of slipping out once he was alone.

He could get dressed on his own, walk on his own, though very slowly. And then walk out of his own front door, which he hadn't done in over a year.

Life was like a roach motel at this point. He had checked in but wasn't able to check out. But that was over. At moments like these, when irrational anger overwhelmed Frank at being cooped up in his house, it was hard not to think of Daniella. All of his girls were good overall, but of course, kids being kids, they'd each had their own behavioral episodes. Regular parenting challenges mostly, all except that one time with Daniella, when the police had to be involved.

It was a few years ago now when Daniella had been fifteen. She was in the second half of her freshman year and had met a boy. *The* boy, apparently. Frank wasn't one of those shotgun-wielding types who tried to keep his daughters little girls forever. Fifteen was a reasonable age to start dating and the boy in question seemed nice. No, the problem was all Daniella's own.

She had barely begun dating when she'd started breaking house rules.

Instead of putting her cell phone in its appointed box at 7 p.m., she'd sneak it into her room and stay up all night, texting. "That wretched boy," he and Bianca used to say. "That boy is leading her astray!" But of course, it was never true.

Then there was the case that instead of coming home straight after school or soccer, she'd go over to Braydon's house as if she had nothing else in her life. Yes, that was his name. Braydon.

Finally, it came to a head. One night, Frank had stormed into the room, taking her phone away for good. And if she wanted to see Braydon, he'd have to come hang out at their house now, wouldn't he? Because Daniella wouldn't be going anywhere but school, Mass, and soccer.

It had seemed an innocent enough plan; she was a teenager, and they were her parents after all. But it had all backfired in a most unanticipated way!

She had exploded in a manner that he could never have expected. Nor did Bianca.

It was like something out of *The Exorcist*.

"This place is a prison and I hate it!" she'd screamed, her face red and blotchy and streaked with the mascara he had also told her she was too young to wear. It had seemed as if she was trying to become a woman, not even in a natural way but as if simply dating meant she thought she *needed* to be someone else. Someone she was not. And he and Bianca didn't like it one bit.

And then at some point, she'd climbed out of her bedroom window and decided to walk to Braydon's house, which was not even in walking distance. That only made it dangerous.

Finding her gone, Bianca had immediately called both Braydon's house—no, they hadn't seen her—and then the police, who found her in short order, bringing her back to the house.

She was still hysterical when they delivered her back in the squad car, but it had turned from vicious screaming to snotty tears by now.

"You don't love me, and you don't want me to be happy! You don't want me to have anything!"

The lovely lady police officer had pulled Bianca aside.

Daniella believed that if she went even one second without contacting Braydon, that he would find a new girlfriend, the officer said. This caused the girl untold anxiety.

As it happened, Braydon's parents had also looked through their son's cell phone and hadn't liked Daniella's obsessive, deranged, and constant text messages one bit. Understandably so.

So, they advised Braydon this wasn't healthy and that it needed to end. Braydon saw their point; there was said to be no arguing from his side; he had seen Daniella's paranoia for himself.

They hadn't demanded it, only advised, at least that was what Braydon's father said to Frank on the phone. Even young Braydon had found Frank's girl way too needy and clingy.

And unfortunately, hearing about the content of the messages, Frank agreed.

Daniella hadn't taken the breakup well at all; it was all the fault of her intrusive, privacy invading parents, she said. She deserved better than that; she was a young woman now.

A woman with her own mind. But that was the point; to Frank and Bianca, she was a teen, a teen who needed care and observation and monitoring, and above all, parental protection. Sure, when she came of age, she could do whatever she liked. Just not yet. They were not there yet.

It had taken her months to go back to even a shadow of civility after that.

He couldn't believe a high school crush had done that to his daughter. But it had.

Meeting Braydon had done this, but they saw it was not his fault; the text messages proved that. But irrespective of the cause, it was like looking at a stranger. A lunatic, even. The formerly sensible girl had departed, and in her place had come a shadow—a dark one at that. How could she think their beautiful home that was so full of love was a prison? How could she throw that at them after everything they had tried to do for her, giving their three wonderful girls such a warm and generous household full of affection and care?

How could some boy she'd only known for a few weeks turn her so violently against her parents? And not even intentionally! How could she be so ungrateful for their love?

"Frank, she's a teenage girl. It's age appropriate that she be hysterical," Bianca had told him once they were alone after the cops brought her back. But he could see she was shaken up by the display too. She didn't think it was normal any more than he did. Together, they were at a loss.

Bianca hadn't said anything at the time, but she later confessed to him that she had even been afraid of Daniella, mostly because of those true-crime murder shows she watched. Several of those cases had been about teenage girls who flipped out and killed their parents.

In every case, they were good girls from respectable families. Straight A students with good friends, and always churchgoers. But then, they met a boy, and they went crazy. Literally. In some cases, the parents forbade the relationship because the boy was older. In one case, the boy ended the relationship—not the parents. But the daughter stabbed her parents to death regardless.

That weighed on Bianca. But she bore that burden alone, only telling Frank about her fears after they'd sent Daniella off to college. There, away from home, she could do whatever she needed to do, and they couldn't be held responsible for it. There, at college, their girl had freedom. And she would make of that newfound freedom whatever she wanted.

Hearing what she had feared, it gave Frank a most peculiar sensation, that of simultaneously thinking his wife had overreacted and also kicking himself for not being more vigilant to the warning signs of violence. If he'd had a son behaving in that unpredictable way, he would have called a therapist that very night for an intervention. No question. A boy acting that erratically—that out of character— was a danger to himself and others. But with a daughter, for some reason, he never imagined violence was even a possibility. Now, he saw that it was.

As he sweltered under his blankets, suffocating in the confines of his bedroom almost in the same way as a banished teenager would have to do, his mind whirred, pondering on it all.

Maybe Daniella hadn't actually hated her home, or her parents.

Perhaps she'd just wanted to be somewhere else, and the lack of freedom to choose that for herself had made her go a bit loopy. Especially with all those raging teenage hormones.

For the first time, he felt as if he understood.

They had never discussed it with her. Never brought it up over the dinner table. There had certainly been no playful barbs about it. "Hey, remember that time you went walking down the street to get to your high school boyfriend? Wasn't that so crazy?" There were plenty of events that hadn't been funny at the time, but they were joked about later.

But Daniella's temporary lunacy was never one of those things. It just seemed easier to pretend it had never happened and that it had no significance in their lives now at all. It was definitely easier to love her the way she deserved if Frank just kept it out of his mind.

That being said, he would have liked to leave her a note before he went off on his adventure. Maybe telling her how she made her mother feel, not just that night, but for a long time afterward. He'd probably also take responsibility for spoiling her a bit. After all, she was the baby of the family. And God knew, even he could have done things differently.

He imagined all three girls had a list of things they'd wished he'd handled better; it wasn't all one-sided. So, fair enough.

But he wouldn't be leaving any notes, not for any of them.

Doing so would only tip off the insurance company that he'd been planning on dying.

In that case, a letter would show it hadn't been just the accidental death of an old man who'd wandered out one day and somehow met a grievous end.

Even if he hid some notes for the girls to find later, long after the investigation closed, he couldn't be sure they wouldn't be honor bound to turn them over. So, no notes. None.

Still, there was a lot he'd like to have said to his daughters. On the other hand, maybe this was a sign some things were better left unsaid. Viviana had once voiced to him, "You don't always get closure on things. And that's okay." She'd been talking about being dumped by a friend with no warning. The girl had just looked at her on the bus one day and said, "I don't want to be friends anymore. Go sit somewhere else." And Viviana, who didn't have many friends, accepted that like a stoic philosopher. "All right," she'd said. "I understand."

Maybe he had something to learn from her. A lot to learn.

He took the remainder of the week to plan out what he would do on Friday, almost as if it was a vacation, though admittedly one from which he would never come back. He had a hard time deciding what he would wear, vacillating between a Hawaiian shirt and cargo shorts—the accepted uniform of elderly dads—and donning his best suit. He would stand out more that way and the shoes would be less comfortable. But he wanted to look good for his last hurrah.

Especially if it was really the way they showed in the movies and one of his daughters would have to identify his body at the morgue. The suit would report to them loud and clear that he'd lived a good last day, not just wandering off in a fit of filth-laden bad hygiene and dementia.

And that same good suit would show he hadn't given up. Hadn't sought an easy exit.

Anyone inquiring or seeing him would think, *here is a fella who lived a very good life, right until the last. One who took care of himself. And vitally, he was enjoying life, every second of it.*

Thus, ruling out any thought of suicide.

Or at least he hoped that was the message they would take away.

First, he would go to Coney Island.

Long Island was far superior, of course, but Coney Island was like a magical fairy land when he was a kid, the ultimate escape. It didn't seem right that he would even contemplate taking a bow and drawing the curtains across his life without going back one more time.

Yes, only after seeing Coney Island and whatever it looked like now would he head back to the old neighborhood. Just thinking about it made his heart pulse faster—just the right mixture of danger and excitement—and he had to make himself calm down in case Samantha came running in to check his pulse. Leaning over to the bedside table, he pulled open the drawer and retrieved a blank index card and a pen. With his scratchy penmanship, he wrote, 'Do Not Resuscitate' on the card and placed it face down back in the drawer.

On Friday, when he went on his last walkabout, he'd put that card into his pocket, muddying it up and bending its corners well and truly first, so it wouldn't appear he'd only just placed it.

It needed to appear as though it had lain in his wallet for a long time.

But whatever the city held for him, whatever shape he was in, whoever found him would know to leave him be. He was ready for his adventure.

The last one he'd ever have.

CHAPTER 7

Waking up Friday morning to an empty house had been a feeling unlike any other. No one yanking at his limbs, no one yelling about what he wanted for breakfast, no one shoving pills down this throat.

No one to see him stumble around, washing and dressing himself for the first time in a year.

Looking at himself in the full-length mirror, Frank smiled, giving his reflection an approving nod. He looked smart enough, though admittedly gaunt and drawn.

He had lost a hell of a lot of weight, his skin hanging off his face like an ill-fitting mask. But the suit still looked reasonably good on him, especially with these well-chosen accessories. Hat, tie pin, cuff links, and watch; Frank would fit in at any convention center. Or Baptist church.

It had been a long time since he'd stood up for that long and he'd had to balance himself against the dresser a few times. But he practiced taking in deep breaths and holding it in, just like his respiratory therapist had taught him, and he was able to stand up without getting dizzy.

Even so, he didn't have the energy to properly make his bed. So, he just pulled the covers up and straightened them. Then he took the opportunity for one last look around the house. The girls' rooms, the living room, the dining room. *So many happy memories.*

One of the girls could move in here, he hoped—maybe Viviana and Pavel. It was ready made to welcome a new baby when one came along.

He really hoped they didn't sell it. But it would be up to them. They were adults now.

In decades past, his inability to drive would have been a problem. But not anymore. All he had to do was call an Uber. A few button pushes and a five-minute wait, and Frank was crawling into the back of a Honda Accord with an Indian kid driving it, not looking any older than sixteen.

"Hello, sir, how are you today, you are having a nice day, huh?" he asked in one long run-on sentence, giving no time to allow the passenger to answer each question.

"I'm doing great… really great," he replied, the words oddly getting caught in his throat. His head turned despite that awkward stiff neck he'd had for some time, and he sighed, catching a last look at his house out the back windshield. *Farewell,* his expression said. *I'll miss you.*

***

Originally, he'd asked the driver to let him off at the boardwalk, but as they drove into Coney Island, there it was, the dome with a cross on top, peeking out from behind the other buildings, and just like that, he changed his mind.

"You okay with dropping me off there?" he asked, pointing at the church, the name of which he couldn't remember.

"Trip still costs the same, sir, yes?" the driver asked, raising his eyebrows in an *are you sure* expression. "No refunds with Uber, you know."

"No. I mean, yes, that's fine."

A few dollars were the last things on his mind.

The church was several blocks away from the boardwalk, but that was okay. He really wanted to go in for some reason.

You feeling guilty, Frankie Boy?

No, that wasn't it. It was more a need to look at something beautiful, to rest someplace quiet before he headed out to the noise of the park. Even though it was early, it was sure to be full of kids and teenagers and loud music and of the course, the relentless noise from the roller coasters. A little reflection time was called for first, that was all.

It was a massive church, one of the old ones.

Our Lady of Solace.

What a perfect name for today.

It wasn't the first time he'd been here, and as he ambled up the brick pathway, the plaque was right there on the path, announcing the rededication in 2015. They'd done some serious work to the church since he was a kid. And he was glad of it. All the new churches looked like convention centers, even the Catholic ones. And Frank didn't want any part of that. Perhaps in some ways, you could say he was progressive, but in many, still held to the old ways.

Couples shouldn't live together before marrying. A man should be the earner in the household. And Catholic churches shouldn't ever look like convention centers or sculptures.

He opened the doors leading into the sanctuary, his eyes wide. Mass was going on.

Only a handful of parishioners were in there, it being a Friday morning, but Frank walked softly so his shoes didn't click and echo against the polished wood floor, taking a seat in the back pew, solemnly listening to the person doing the reading.

"See what love the Father has bestowed on us by letting us be called children of God…"

Frank craned his neck to look at the gorgeous arched ceiling above the altar, the original mosaic pattern he remembered from his youth still intact.

The floor had been refinished, the altar replaced. The pews were new, obviously, and maybe some of the stained-glass windows were also different, though it was hard to be sure.

This was a building in which you were meant to feel the spirit. And it accomplished its task. His family had never been members here; they went to St. Joseph's, of course, the parish for their neighborhood. But every once in a while, when his ma brought him to the park, she would take a minute to pop in here to light a candle. For what, he didn't know. But she never lit one when they went to Mass as a family. Just here, at someone else's church.

And sometimes, she brought Frank with her.

It had been a mostly Irish neighborhood back then.

Every time he'd come in with his mother, it had been a sea of blondes and light browns, plus more freckles than should ever reasonably gather in one place.

But now, it looked to be a mostly Spanish neighborhood. Not Puerto Ricans either. Maybe the good people in the pews had come from Central America originally.

There were so many groups in New York now, it was hard to say. He spoke Italian, and Spanish wasn't that different, so he could get by talking to the Spanish speakers. Well, with Mexicans and Colombians, anyway. Puerto Ricans, on the other hand, not so much.

They talked so fast and had so much slang, Frank could barely make heads or tails of what they were saying. But they were good Catholics, just like him. And that was what mattered.

A lot of boys would get pulled aside by their fathers around puberty to hear about the birds and the bees. Frank got a quick and ugly rundown of the procedure, but right afterwards, his father had eyed his son seriously, saying, "When you want to get married, you can come home with any kind of Catholic girl you want. Irish girl, Puerto Rican, even one of them Korean Catholics. Just don't dare come home with a Protestant, Frankie. Don't do that to your mother."

Being twelve at the time, the request—no, the mandate —had taken him off guard. His best friend, Vinny, had already gotten the *birds and bees* talk from his old man and he'd told Frankie all about it. His pop had given him a dirty magazine and a cigarette, telling him if he was good, then next year, he'd bring him someplace where he could learn to 'do it' firsthand.

That was kind of what Frank had been hoping for. But no such luck. He just got a lecture about not bringing home any Protestant girls.

It turned out to not be a hard promise to keep. Even with his doubts about the Catechism springing up early and often, Frank didn't spend his time with Protestants. Not the boys or the girls. They just acted different. They were loud and acted as though the Bible was something made specially for them. It was off-putting. So, he naturally gravitated to other Catholics.

He didn't even need to ask who was who. He just knew.

And when he saw Bianca Calderone getting on his bus that day in her candy striped uniform, he'd known at first sight that this was the girl he would marry.

And that she was a Catholic girl his mother would love.

A chill swept over Frank, and he hunched over in the pew, pulling his baggy suit jacket closer to his body. Looking around, no one else in the church seemed cold at all.

Must be all the weight I've lost. But he was lying to himself. He took the folded handkerchief from his front pocket and wiped his brow, covered in sweat despite the fact that he was freezing. He should probably get going, but didn't want to get up yet.

They were just getting to the homily, his favorite part of the Mass.

He had never been super religious, unlike Bianca. But regardless, Christianity was the best formula to follow to be a good man, so he'd stuck with it. Bianca had had a lot to say about 'Cafeteria Catholics' when they talked privately, getting so fired up about people who didn't follow the religion to the letter. Maybe it was out of genuine concern for their souls though.

If there was one thing Bianca wasn't, it was controlling. She didn't have a mean or manipulative bone in her body; even when she got mad, she was always nice about it.

"Frank, I am very, very upset with you right now. I asked you to call me from work at noon and you didn't. I was late picking up Viviana from school and I was *so* embarrassed, felt as if you don't care enough to listen to me."

Everything Frank had ever been told about 'productive conflict' at those stupid seminars at work, Bianca just did naturally.

For sure, that was the light of God shining through her. She had it burning in her like a flame.

And she could see it in others too, even when it didn't exactly shine so brightly.

Frank, on the other hand…

Let's just say he had to work hard at seeing the light of God in people.

He waited until people started getting up to go take communion to make his exit. He wouldn't be taking it with them. Even if he hadn't been planning on hurrying his eventual death along, he hadn't been to confession in decades. It wouldn't be right to take the Sacrament. Given the circumstances, maybe God would let it slide just this once. But even if He did, Bianca wouldn't. And he'd have to answer to her in the afterlife just as much as to God.

Assuming he got to heaven, that was.

He wasn't afraid of hell so much as he feared being separated from Bianca.

Part of why he hurt so much for Annabella was his personal knowledge of how it felt to be cut off from the person you loved most. But at least he had the assurance that Bianca wanted him just as much as he'd always craved her. She'd had her pick of fellas and somehow, though he would never quite grasp why, she had chosen him. Though Lord knew, he'd made her regret it a time or two, something for which he would never stop being sorry.

That had been the first time he'd gone years without taking communion. He had wronged Bianca, you see, and it would take more than a few *Hail Mary's* to make that right.

So, he'd taken his time before going back up to that communion rail. He might not believe in everything in the Catechism. But he believed in penance. That was for damn sure.

Breathing hard, Frank walked out of the sanctuary, back down the brick path toward the main sidewalk. But on the last step, his leg grew jittery, then buckled beneath him, sending him crashing to the ground, his shoulder radiating pain as he landed hard on it.

A couple walked right by him, iced coffees in hand, not even a look in his direction.

What the hell's happened to this city?

Yeah, New Yorkers had always been assholes, but they hadn't been like that.

He tried to ease himself up, only for the rest of his body to lock up on him.

The chill that had fled from his body had been replaced by an unbearable, scorching heat. With a gasp, his body was starting to flail, completely out of his control. He couldn't stop his limbs from shaking, or his head from flopping. He couldn't even close his eyes and wait for the inevitable moment when he would crack open his head on the pavement.

That would be a good way to go, Lord. Please let this be it. Just let me not feel it.

As if in answer, the seizing stopped and Frank was left gasping on the sidewalk, every muscle in his body screaming in pain. He had definitely hit his head.

But not hard enough to do serious damage. At least he didn't think so.

And still, even as he was having a whole seizure at the entrance to a church, no one stopped to ask if he was okay. No one called him an ambulance.

Good. I don't need one of those anyway. He checked his pocket to make sure the note card that said *Do Not Resuscitate* was still there. And it was.

Then, with great care and even greater effort, Frank got back up and walked slowly away from the church, headed for the Coney Island boardwalk.

CHAPTER 8

It was a Friday morning during the school year, but the Coney Island boardwalk was packed. Frank beamed as he felt the adrenaline shoot through him, the sights and sounds of his childhood and his time as a young man flooding back.

This. This was why his last day would be here. The place was alive! He hadn't left his house in over a year. Hell, he hadn't even left his bedroom. It had been one day after another of his daughters' sadness and the ministrations of the nurse who had been paid to watch him until he eventually died. It made him feel as if he was already dead.

But not today.

Bells, whistles, clangs, the mechanized sound of coins dropping onto metal, and the joyous laughter of children. Everything here teemed with life, reminding him of why he used to get up in the morning and why he'd looked forward to going through the hassle of taking the girls out here when they were little. The colors, the smells, and the energy that seemed to make the air vibrate weren't like anything else in the world.

With the breeze in his face, Frank smiled as he watched the families go by—mothers and their gaggle of kids, couples with their sullen teenagers, and an enormous number of unaccompanied youngsters. It was good parents still let kids wander around beaches and piers.

At least as far as he was concerned.

What to do first?

He stopped walking so he could turn in a circle, getting the lay of the land and seeing what had changed in the years since he'd last been here. It seemed louder, that was for sure.

It felt as if the vendors were now competing against the rides instead of existing alongside them, noise and color exploding out of every space in rapid succession. Massive clouds of pink spun sugar hung from the rafters of the booths alongside stuffed animals, and every kind of candy you could imagine stood out from baskets and racks in wild, bright colors. It was all like a beckoning hand with a carnival voice barking out, "come and get some!"

The smell of cooking meat made Frank's mouth water —hot dogs, or a chopped cheese sandwich? That was the question. The scintillating flavors of grease, beef, and pork—or whatever else was in hot dogs—competed for his attention and brought him back to the days of high metabolism when he could have both those treats in a single day and suffer for it later.

He hadn't had either in so long, and Samantha would have a fit if she saw him even looking at a chopped cheese. But Samantha wasn't here, and it was his last day, after all.

What was a little bout of heartburn in the grand scheme of things?

"Damn old man, you on your way to church or something?"

A chorus of laughter echoed the question as three boys brushed past Frank, knocking him out of his internal debate over snacks.

"Nah, I went to see your mother. She wants me to look nice for her," Frank shot back at the kid, whose smile dropped immediately when his friends' laughter now turned on him.

Frank smiled in victory as the kids kept moving down the boardwalk, the loudmouth one looking more confused than angry.

What, did the kids not tell 'your mother' jokes anymore?

Wearing his suit, Frank stood out like a sore thumb, but so far, the one kid was the only one who seemed to notice. No one else stared or even spared him a passing glance. Instead, they went about their way in the eclectic mix of jeans, cargo pants, and what looked like pajamas to Frank, but were probably referred to as 'athletic attire' in the stores.

A distant roar filled his ears and Frank forgot all about the enticing aroma of beef on a grill.

If he was going to eat anything, it needed to be later.

First, he wanted to ride the roller coaster. And if there was one thing he remembered from boyhood, it was that you were supposed to eat *after* the roller coaster. Not before it. Probably some other poor souls had learned that the hard way too, thanks to young Frank.

Straightening his out-of-place suit jacket, Frank made his way over to the roller coaster—an institution, a monument even, called the Cyclone. The massive wooden roller coaster had been there when he was a boy, and he was heartened to see it still standing strong.

It was an oddly incongruous thought, however, that he was worn out and needing to be dismantled, figuratively speaking, while this old boyhood amusement would outlive him by far. It was strange how, when you were a kid, such things would never even cross your mind.

The older you got, the faster time raced—though for Frank, still not fast enough.

Even though his old man had always hated roller coasters, he'd agreed to ride it with him once, though he'd been pretty green around the gills when they were done.

Frank looked up at the slope, craning his neck and squinting against the sun. He could feel the vibrations of the coaster in his feet even though it was on the other side of the ride. As he looked down, his gaze narrowed in on a hammer lying near the tracks.

Why was there always debris around roller coaster tracks?

He remembered the very first time he'd ridden the roller coaster, and even then, there nails all over the place, which had freaked Frank out. Well, maybe these things just weren't safe, always needing a load of repairs.

Hmm. That set him to thinking.

Perhaps he should go on one, though it would be just Frank's luck that he'd end up sick, not dead, and that a raging torrent of nausea would prevent him continuing his quest for the exit with a capital E. So, maybe not.

Or at least, a roller coaster ride ought to be a last resort, no pun intended.

As a kid, he'd come to the park with Carlo Sanguinetti, an older boy from the neighborhood. Their mothers had been friends, so Mom had let him come this time with no adults, which was fantastic. But then when Carlo had dared him to ride the Cyclone, he hadn't been crazy about it.

"What about those nails?" He'd pointed at the rusty metal pieces scattered on the tracks.

The older boy had laughed at him.

"If you're scared, Frankie boy, just say so. You can stay down here and watch me have the time of my life up there. With them." He'd pointed to a group of pretty girls standing in line, laughing and squealing at each other as they saw Carlo pointing at them.

"I'm not scared!" Frank had shot back. "I'm just saying it looks dangerous. What if it makes the cart go off the tracks?"

"It won't," grumbled Carlo, grabbing him by the collar and dragging him into the line. Not at the end either. He cut right in front of the girls, gave the red-headed one a wink, and said, "Thanks for holding our spot, beautiful."

When the giggling died down and Carlo had gotten the names and phone numbers of every girl in the group, he'd leaned down and whispered in Frank's ear, "They'd have to pay a lot of money if anyone got hurt on their ride. Trust me, kid. They're not gonna let anyone get hurt."

And he was right. He and Carlo had ridden that roller coaster at least thirty times that day and never had a single incident. The nails stayed where they were but didn't cause a problem.

But now, decades later, it was a hammer. Not on the tracks, but awfully close to them. What if *that* ended up on the tracks? What would it do to the roller coaster?

Derail it? Send it careening off the edge? Now all grown up, Frank knew Carlo had been right about the big payout if the park was negligent and people got hurt. So, if there were a way for him to sneak onto the tracks—make sure that hammer did end up where it would cause a problem— maybe the girls would get an additional payout for negligence.

Frank shook the thought out of his head, not liking the selfishness of that image.

The hammer wasn't close enough to cause a problem, which was a good thing. As the coaster rushed past, the excited screams of the people aboard it rang in his ears. They were all just here to have a good time. And there was no way his will to die superseded anyone else's will to live.

Not just their will either. Their God-given right.

And as a man of faith, how could God reward Frank's kids if he offed himself only by taking half a dozen others along with him? Or even if it turned out to be just one person he maimed.

That was the thing about killing yourself. To do it right, you had to *only* kill yourself. Sure, playing around with a roller coaster would make it look like an accident. But even if there were only one other person on the ride… that was one too many. He didn't want anyone else to get hurt. Causing a car crash meant the same thing—endangering people who didn't deserve it.

Well, damn. He'd planned his last day of fun, but he'd left the method of how the day would end up to chance. He would have to think about the way he would make his exit carefully.

There was no denying Frank had been selfish in his life from time to time. Well, one long stretch of time specifically. And the thought of his span of selfishness still made him sick.

So, he wouldn't be signing up for that again, certainly not in his last moments, when judgment was coming. No, he absolutely would not do anything that could hurt anyone else. Instead, he pushed away from the railing and got in the long line for the Cyclone.

He would just ride the coaster one last time. Like he used to. For fun only.

The line was long, and Frank's whole body hurt. Every shuffling step he took when the line moved seemed to make it worse. He'd brought a few pills with him for just such an occasion. After reading all the websites on what would happen if he stopped his medication, stopping cold turkey had turned out to be a no-go too.

He'd just taper off enough to keep a clear head. But the pain, that was still there. And if he was going to make it all the way through his day, he needed a pick-me-up.

He reached into his pocket and pulled out the orange-brown bottle, his hands shaking slightly as he twisted the cap off and popped one in his mouth.

He didn't have any water, so the pill was bitter and took several painful swallows to get that damn thing to go down. If he were a hard-ass type, he'd chew it.

But he couldn't bear it; the taste was too bad. And if anything, the powdery chewed-up pill was even harder to swallow once you bit down on it.

He promised himself he'd get a bottle of water when he got off the ride. For the next pill.

Finally, the long line brought him up to the tracks, the pill mercifully kicking in, giving him a warm buzz and a soothing relief in his back and neck.

Once seated and buckled in, the roller coaster started off slow, clicking and jerking around the first bend before gaining momentum, intent on making its way up the first steep incline.

Frank's guts were twisting and tightening in excitement.

Carlo had made such a show of daring him to come on the Cyclone. And he had, loving every minute of it, riding it seven times in a row before they took a break to get some food. That was something his mother never would have allowed. Probably why she was happy for him to go with Carlo.

Now, decades later and sitting next to complete strangers, Frank had that bizarre sense of déjà vu, staring down the same hill, feeling his head spin at being up so high. Had he made a mistake?

If you have a heart attack, all the better.

He felt his stomach drop as they rushed down, all screaming in unison, the kids' high-pitched voices mixing with the grownups in an exhilarating crescendo.

His body jerked from side to side around each corner, the vibrations on the ride feeling as though they just might shake him apart, the air rushing past him in a cool hurricane. And just like that, it was over. After going around the last curve, the car slowed just enough to safely jolt to a stop, having delivered to Frank the most glorious few minutes he'd had in a long time.

He sat in the car for a bit, too dizzy to get up immediately. Lucky for him, he wasn't the only one who was wobbly. The shrieking girls in front were holding hands, helping one another onto the platform, laughing about how dizzy they were. Gripping tightly to every surface within reaching distance, Frank got out of the car, onto the platform and, with the help of the railing, he followed the line all the way back to the entrance, smiling ear to ear.

As he walked free of the fence surrounding the ride, Frank looked around, trying to decide where he'd go next, his days of riding the Cyclone multiple times in a row far behind him. But as he tried to take another step toward one of the concession vendors, his legs started quaking beneath him, his knees feeling as if they would collapse out from under him.

Get out of the crowd! he thought, frantically looking around as the shaking spread to the rest of his body, sweat dripping off his face and onto his collar, soaking through his shirt. Frank found his way to a bench on which no one else sat just as the convulsions started in earnest.

Gritting his teeth, he desperately battled for control over his body, trying to get the shaking to stop or even to lessen, but he was helpless. His heart rate skyrocketed, and his chest constricted.

So helpless was he that he couldn't even wrest control of his arms enough to loosen his collar. He couldn't breathe!

As the quaking of his body propelled him off the bench and onto the concrete, Frank waited for the moment his head would crack against the ground and it would all be over.

You'll be with Bianca soon. You'll see. Just get through this, then her arms will hold you.

But Bianca never did come. Instead, in place of his sweet lifetime love, scrapes and bangs assailed his limbs and his head, but none hard enough to make a severe injury. The seizure seemed to go on forever and forever, until, slowly but surely, the convulsions stopped.

With a deep breath, he filled his lungs, right before laying his head back and passing out in exhaustion.

CHAPTER 9

One thing they never show you in the movies when someone wakes from a faint is the dry heaving. Almost everyone who fainted, upon waking up, would be wracked with nausea spasms. Luckily for Frank, he hadn't gotten that chopped cheese, so his stomach was empty when it started to twist—almost as soon as he opened his eyes.

Without the energy to bolt upright, he managed to twist to the side as he heaved three times, a chill taking over him.

Once it was done, he breathed in deeply, blinking several times, trying to orient himself.

I'm at Coney Island. I rode the Cyclone.

"Hey buddy, you all right?"

Still lying on the ground, propped up on one elbow, Frank sighed internally. He must have looked ridiculous to the people walking all around him.

Feeling his face get hot, he pushed himself into a sitting position, looking toward the male voice that had called out to him.

Squinting against the sun, he looked up to see a thick, broad-shouldered man—around Frank's age and also wearing a suit, oddly enough—leaning down with his hands on his knees, concern wrinkling his face.

"You need an ambulance or something? Or are you just having a senior moment? No need to be embarrassed, I tripped on my way to the can just last night. It's hell getting old."

The man broke out into a laugh and recognition shot through Frank.

"Carlo? Carlo Sanguinetti?" he asked, squinting to make sure he hadn't made a mistake. Could it be him, after all these years?

The smile dropped from the man's face, which he then contorted into an exaggerated squint as he studied Frank's face in return. It only took him a second to recognize him.

"Fightin' Frank Vitale! How the hell are you, kid?"

He thrust out a meaty hand, which Frank gladly took to steady himself as he got to his feet.

"Not a kid anymore, as you can see," he said, smiling from ear to ear.

The two regarded each other, Carlo probably having the same thoughts as Frank. How long had it been? Fifteen years since they'd last spoken, was it? Had to be, at least.

Longer than that since they'd seen each other in person.

"You look… different," Carlo said, not bothering to keep the concerned look off his face, taking in Frank's desiccated appearance.

"Yeah, you too," Frank said, going out of his way not to let his eyes linger on Carlo's flabby and swinging jowls. He didn't need to, of course.

"Well, I got fat. What are you gonna do?" Carlo asked, holding his arms out to the side, making it clear he'd enjoyed every single plate of food that got him to his newfound size, and he had zero regrets. But even with the weight, Carlo looked great. His tan suit was expertly tailored, the bright purple shirt and coordinating tie underneath shining in the sun.

Now, here was a man not out to try and kill himself. Not that Frank looked as if he had death on his day's agenda either. But Carlo—he wore that suit flamboyantly.

It wasn't a look Frank would ever sport himself, but he could respect flashiness on others. And he sure respected him right now, particularly since he knew what Carlo did for a living.

"So, what are you doing on the ground, Frankie boy? One of these punk kids push you over or something?" Carlo asked, looking around them with his eyebrows up, as if he was about to snatch a random teenager and give him a talking to. Maybe even a punch in the mouth.

"Nah, nothing like that," Frank said, brushing dirt from his jacket and taking note of his Brooklyn accent returning in force. "Just got dizzy for a second. These damn pills, y'know?"

Carlo laughed, giving his old buddy a hefty slap on the back.

"Yeah, I do. My doc tried to get me on blood pressure pills last year, but they stopped my pecker from working. I might be old, but I'm not dead, so I told him no thanks! What brings you here? You got grandkids?"

He whipped his head around, eyes low to the pavement, obviously seeking out Frank's mystery grandchildren.

"Nah, not yet. My middle one's married and they're making plans that way. But none yet. How about you?" he asked, sidestepping the question entirely.

Carlo held his hands out, his face in a familiar grimace. "Well, I just came to see someone. One of the old gang runs some of the concessions if you know what I mean."

He tapped at the side of his nose.

Frank did know, too. Frank knew all about Carlo and the life he lived. It was the reason they hadn't spoken in almost two decades. But he was so glad to see him, even though he was still living that life… at his age. Of all people he could have run into—all the people he could have reconnected with and made it right—honestly, Frank was glad it was Carlo Sanguinetti.

They'd grown up together. Well, kind of. Carlo was three years older than Frank, and that was a lot when you were a kid, so they hadn't ever played together.

But Carlo was always good, a kid whose word meant something in the neighborhood.

Once, Frank got into a fight with Patrick Finnegan, who was also an older kid, and a hell of a lot faster and stronger than Frank. At the time, he had just turned sixteen, which made him a little too old to be getting into stupid tussles. But everyone knew Patrick was a real prick and liked to push other kids around. And one day while walking home from school, Patrick decided it was Frank's turn to be picked on. Well, he'd had it easy for a time, had Frank.

Yeah, he could have put up with it. He could have just kept his head down and hurried home after Patrick lobbed a rock at Frank's head and called him a fag. Maybe he should have.

Because Patrick knew how to fight.

His old man was a boxer and Frank had never been too keen on getting into fights. But that day, he dove in with a roar, even though he knew in advance he would lose. He'd rather have his ass kicked up one side of Brooklyn and down the other than be seen backing down from a bully.

So, he'd been prepared for a fat lip and a black eye. But Patrick had a lot more than that in mind. Even after it was clear Frank had lost the fight, Patrick kept coming.

The punches kept landing on Frank, on his face, his gut, and he even got slammed in the ear a couple times and the rage on Patrick's face made it clear he wouldn't be stopping.

The little shit had a real problem with some Italian kid having the stones to stand up to him.

Frank thought it would have gone real bad that day. But then Carlo jumped in, pulling Patrick off and daring him to pull that crap with someone his own size.

Carlo was a short guy but built like a brick shit house. And unlike Frank, Carlo made a habit of fighting, and it was well known his father was a made man—a mobster.

So, he heaved Patrick off of Frank and when he told the red-headed prick to get lost, he did. The kid knew better than to pick a brutal fight with a mobster's lad. There'd be only one way that could have ended up, and let's just say that Carlo wouldn't have been the loser.

Even the son of an Irish boxer knew better than to screw around with a mobster's kid.

Frank's ears were ringing, and he couldn't breathe through his nose.

Everything hurt like hell and his mom was going to flip out when he got home. At least he didn't think he was missing any teeth.

Once Patrick had gone, Carlo helped him up and walked him home, even though he was dressed as if on his way somewhere fancy.

"That was ballsy what you did back there, Frankie. What are you doing when you're done with school? Maybe gonna be a cop?"

Frank had laughed, spraying blood out of his mouth. "Nah, not me. I'll probably work at the factory with my dad."

Carlo had turned, casting him a look as if that was the stupidest thing he had ever heard. "Nah, you can do better than that."

"You saying factories ain't good work?" Frank asked, a little defensive at the implication.

"I'm saying a factory ain't good for everyone. Probably ain't good for you."

When they turned the corner onto Frank's street, Carlo had taken a handkerchief out of his pocket and dabbed at

Frank's face a bit, trying to make him a little more presentable. "If I were you, I wouldn't tell your ma who done this to your face. Last time an Italian kid fought an Irish kid, their mothers ended up getting into a fight at the church."

Frank laughed again, but it was cut short by the pain that ripped through his face. "Yeah, I remember that. And Father Mallinson threatened to excommunicate the both of them."

They laughed at the memory, though it was definitely one of those things that wasn't funny at the time.

"Anyway, thanks for helping me out. You didn't have to," said Frank.

"No one *has to* do anything," Carlo said and shrugged. "That's the beauty of it. You get to choose who you are."

It was such a basic thing to say, but Frank had been struck by the phrase.

He stood dumbfounded, watching Carlo walk away. And now, decades later, he remembered it as if it was yesterday. That phrase, *you don't have to do anything,* had made it clear to Frank that he got to choose his own destiny. He got to choose how he reacted to things.

He got to choose who he became; there was nothing pre-determined, and just because his father worked in a factory, it didn't mean Frank also had to. He needed to make his own decisions, and it was just a matter of being willing to accept the consequences.

And so, that was what Frank did. There and then, he chose to live a good life and marry a good woman. Carlo… he'd chosen to do something else.

"Well, come on and sit down over here with me, Frank," Carlo said, steering him over toward the closest bench. "How's Bianca, by the way? She come with you today?"

As they walked toward the bench, Carlo's phone, clipped to his belt, lit up and rang, the name NICKY on the screen.

In one smooth motion, Carlo looked down, made a face when he saw the name, and pressed the button to send the call to voicemail.

"You got work to do—"

"It's not important, Frankie boy," Carlo, said, sitting on the bench beside him. "How's Bianca?"

"She died, actually," he said, his voice low and turning hoarse at that terrible sentence. "Last year. I still miss her, Carlo. She was my only real love."

Carlo's full face went slack, shock and sadness wiping all traces of joviality from his eyes. "God, Frankie, I'm so sorry. What happened? Do you mind me asking? Was it cancer?"

Frank swallowed hard. He hadn't been prepared to talk about this today. Hadn't been prepared to talk about anything, really. Just see the sights and pick a way to go to the great beyond. But now Carlo was here. Never really a friend, but perhaps the person he'd known the longest outside of family. Carlo from the neighborhood, the one who knew exactly what Frank was about, and who had known exactly how wonderful Bianca had been.

So, he took a deep breath. "It wasn't cancer," he said. And he told him all about what happened. The accident. The coma. The full-time nurse. And his escape on this day.

He left out only one thing, and that was how he planned to end the day.

The whole time, Carlo never wavered in his attention, never let his eyes wander away or reached down to check his phone. He listened with rapt attention, only moving to put a hand on Frank's shoulder. "She was a good woman, Frank. I'm sorry that happened. Your girls are still good though, right? Bianca lives on in the girls too, you know. Never forget that."

It was a surreal moment, Carlo, the mobster's boy, almost whispering soft, reassuring words.

Frank nodded. "Yeah. I know, and the girls are more than good. How about your boys?"

Carlo laughed and Frank gave him a cheeky smile, both of them silently acknowledging Carlo's unusual family arrangement.

Though Frank had had one wife and three daughters, Carlo had also worked his way through four wives that Frank knew of, and had produced no fewer than eleven kids. All. Boys.

"Ah, they're doing what they're doing. My youngest… you believe he's the one that made me proud? He's only nineteen and making more money than his three closest brothers combined. Making computer games about knights for gaming nerds or some shit. You wouldn't believe how much money he makes! Got his own place and everything. It took me a minute… you know, I wanted him to go to college. But he's doing good. I'm proud of him. The rest of 'em…" he made a so-so gesture with his hand. "They're getting by, I suppose."

Frank nodded, glad to hear Carlo's kids were doing well, at least some of them. Say what you wanted about Carlo's business practice, he took being a father seriously. It was telling that of the eleven sons, only two had gotten into 'the life' and expressly against Carlo's wishes. But once they grew up, as Frank knew perfectly well, kids were always going to do what they wanted.

You could try and steer them the right way, whatever that was, but they made their own lives.

And that was a good thing, wasn't it? No man wanted kids depending on him too much.

Carlo took a handkerchief out of his pocket, dabbing sweat from his forehead. It wasn't hot out, but Carlo was mildly winded, making Frank feel a hell of a lot better about his own frailty.

"Listen, Frankie, I don't have anything important on tap today. So, what do you say—want to make a day of it? Like old times?"

As soon as the offer was out of Carlo's mouth, Frank felt a smile spread across his face. The only thing that gave him pause was exactly how long he could go on having someone around. Having Carlo nearby might stop him from taking an opportunity to end things if one came along.

But looking at his old friend's face, he couldn't bear the thought of saying no. Just couldn't.

How long had it been since he'd just had a day with one of the guys? And one from the old neighborhood at that? He couldn't think of a better way to spend his last day out. Plus, if he declined to accept and then he found his exit strategy, that would make Carlo feel really bad.

But hopefully, if they had a good day together, Carlo could take some solace from that.

"Sure, Carlo. That would be swell," he heard himself say.

CHAPTER 10

It's probably not a common sight at an amusement park, two old guidos in suits playing skee-ball on a Friday afternoon.

"You remember it ever being this tiring?" Frank laughed, trying to cover the clicking sound his shoulder made as he lobbed the ball up the ramp, relishing the sound of the bell and the flashing red lights as the ball sailed into the hole marked 50.

"Still got it!" he laughed, pumping his fist in the air.

"Yeah, you do," Carlo said, clutching onto the ridiculous pink bear he'd won in the last round. Overweight he might have been, but Carlo was in far better shape than Frank and his arm was a veritable cannon. Just like when they'd been kids.

"You remember when we weren't allowed to play this on Sundays? Never knew what that was about," said Carlo, sailing the ball into the 30 hole.

"Some places called it gambling back then because it's classified as a redemption game, so they shut it down on Sundays. But it's hard to rig, so I say it's not gambling. Luckily, New York and New Jersey came around to thinking that too. The odds of playing a perfect game are still pretty high. Especially at our age."

"Always you with the probability," Carlo laughed. "Always weighing things up."

"Hey, it's what I do," Frank said, rubbing his shoulder while Carlo took a turn at the ramp.

But it was true, young Frank Vitale had been blessed with a good brain. Sure, he'd always imagined he would end up a factory worker, the way his father was. Or maybe if he was feeling aspirational, he would have said he wanted to be a mechanic. Maybe even an aircraft mechanic.

That was what he really wanted because the good money was to be had by doing that.

Or what he thought good money was.

But he didn't grow up to work with his hands, of course. In an interesting twist of fate, Frank had grown up to be an actuary. Interesting because if he had gone back in time and told his younger self what lay in store for him, young Frankie probably would have responded, "What the hell is an actuary?" And so would most other people, even the adults.

An actuary was basically someone who looked at statistics, then looked at you, and based on how you fit into those statistics, he would decide how much you were going to pay in insurance premiums. An upper-class white man who drove a white sedan and didn't smoke? That'd be a nice low bill for you, my friend. Black guy in a sports car who smoked endless Newports?

Sorry, fella. But you're gonna be paying a fair bit more. Even though statistically, you make less money per year. It wasn't fair, but it was a living.

Numbers had always come easily to Frank.

The teachers at school had marveled at how quickly he snapped up the math lessons, how he did his homework in class while the teacher was still talking, and then pleaded for more. To him, numbers were comfort; they just made sense. It was a fun party trick; people would ask him complicated arithmetic problems at parties and Frank would solve them. Then the movie *Rain Man* came out, and they compared him to Dustin Hoffman's character.

Frank would just laugh it off, but it chapped his ass if he was honest, hardly a favorable comparison. Anyway, how funny that it was a fight with his dad that got him on the path to the career to make his whole life possible. His comfortable upper middle-class life, meeting Bianca, getting a nice house in the suburbs, and later, having their wonderful three girls.

And all because his old man had forbidden him from putting in for an insurance job.

Frank had just graduated from high school and was looking for work. Obviously, his dad had brought him by the factory to show him the ropes, and he was willing to give it a try, but he wanted to look for other opportunities first. Something a little less… well, mindless.

An ad in the paper had been seeking an insurance clerk, asking for no experience and the ability to learn quickly. It sounded interesting. Frank told his dad he was going to put in for it. His father would be proud, wouldn't he? A clerk was a good job, one that was decent.

"Not that one, Frankie," Paul snarled. "That's a woman's job. No boy of mine's going to be a clerk, so get that out of your head."

Still being the clueless kid he was, Frank held up the newspaper to show him. "Pop, look it's a clerk. It's under the *men's help wanted.* Not *women's help wanted.*"

Paul just slapped the paper away, not even looking at the ad. "It's a secretary! They're gonna have you typing and filing. Is that how I raised you? Did that school turn you into a fanook?"

Without hesitation, Frank had popped his old man right in the face.

No forethought, no planning, the terror of anyone overhearing him being accused of being gay enough to make him strike his own father.

His hand just shot out and cracked Paul Vitale in the mouth, knocking his head back and drawing blood from his lip.

Shocked at himself but shaking in anger, Frank had yelled, "You want me to be a nothing, don't you Dad, just like you!"

The look his father gave him didn't need any words to go with it.

Get out and don't come back.

And he did. There was no need for more words between them.

Needless to say, that was the last night Frank ever stayed in that house. He was eighteen years old, old enough to go to war, and old enough not to put up with being talked to like that, that was for damn sure. He was also old enough to realize that his father's insistence on him working at the factory had nothing to do with him worrying about Frank being thought of as gay.

Even living out of a suitcase, Frank got the insurance clerk job.

The manager was so thrilled with him, he promptly went out to the lobby to shoo away two other applicants. And though it was kind of hard on the other two, that small action made Frank feel so great, even with the weight of being kicked out of his house on his shoulders.

The job brought along with it a fair amount of typing and filing just as his dad had rudely said, but Frank didn't mind at all, relishing the orderliness of it. He loved talking to the customers, loving his boss too. There was nothing bad about it.

Plus, it was double what his father made right out the gate. Which was probably why he hadn't wanted Frank to take the job in the first place. But this job only brought great things, two happening in close succession. The first was his boss noticing Frank's aptitude for numbers, enrolling him in an actuarial course. And only a month after that, he met Bianca on a bus. From then on, that was his life. Bianca, and calculating probabilities.

The red lights flashed again, Carlo's last ball sinking into the 50 hole now, sending a deluge of tickets pouring from the machine.

"All right, I don't think my knees can take much more of this," Carlo said, groaning as he pulled the tickets out. "You been to the aquarium lately?"

Frank narrowed his eyes. "Actually, no. It was on my list of things to do today."

Carlo nodded, then jerked his head. "Well let's go see it then. I wanna see the seals."

Frank nodded again, this time with something akin to suspicion.

He followed Carlo silently, watching him as he handed the bear he'd won to a kid passing by, giving the boy instructions to pass it on to a pretty girl.

"Gotta help these kids with their game," he said, talking over his shoulder. "They spend so much time buried in their phones, they don't know how to make the first move. Hate to see it."

Frank smiled, unable to help himself. But as they walked across the park toward the exit, he had a strange feeling, telling him that running into Carlo wasn't an accident.

Did God send him? Or Bianca?

Are you trying to tell me not to do this, honey? Is that why you sent him?

It just seemed to be too big a coincidence. Especially since the last time they'd talked, Carlo hadn't been happy with Frank at all.

It had hurt when they'd fallen out. It couldn't be helped, but it was a sad day when he'd told Carlo never to call him again, and that hurt had carried on all these years. Who would have thought that two grown-ass men could have such a falling out like a pair of schoolkids?

So why had Carlo looked so happy to see him?

Why hadn't he demanded an apology or mentioned their falling out? It was unusual.

But they were having a good time, weren't they?

And Frank didn't want to bring it up. What'd be the point?

This was Frank's last day, and it was a well-known fact that people were supposed to settle all their arguments before they died. Carlo just happening to cross paths with Frank today was a timely blessing, a gift offering both men a chance to put the past firmly where it belonged.

They exited the amusement park, both of them huffing and puffing throughout the long walk across the street and then the parking lot separating the park from the aquarium, the tall aqua-green entrance gate beckoning in the distance.

Though his fondest memories of this place were from when he was a kid, he and Bianca used to take the girls to the aquarium when they were younger. He'd been a teenager when they'd built the place, and by then he'd been far too interested in cars and girls to spend much time there. Just as well, he supposed. It hadn't looked nearly as grand in those days as it did now.

"I got this, Frank," said Carlo, pulling out his wallet as they approached the window at the entrance. This time, when Frank nodded, he felt his heart skip in his chest and he lost his balance, keeling over into a potted plant lining the walkway.

"Jesus, Frank!" Carlo abandoned the payment window, diving forward to catch him.

"I'm fine—"

"The hell you are. We ain't seen each other in a while, but you think I didn't notice how much weight you lost? That ain't from being on a diet so don't bullshit a bullshitter."

He tugged Frank over to the side, away from the families waiting in line, some of whom had turned to look. With Carlo heaving him by the armpits onto a bench, Frank felt his head loll back against the wall. "Just need another pill."

"Where they at?" Carlo demanded.

"Jacket pocket."

Without another word, Carlo shoved his hand into Frank's pocket, pulling out the dark bottle and shaking a few tablets into his hand.

"One or two? You want me to get you a soda or something?"

"Just the one pill," Frank said, grabbing it from Carlo's hand and chewing it up, powering through the bitter, disgusting taste flooding his mouth and throat as he swallowed it. He never did answer about the drink. Carlo stood and grimaced at his pal's way of downing the vile pill.

As he waited for his equilibrium to settle back into place, Frank sucked in deep breaths through his nose, willing himself not to have another seizure. Mercifully, he didn't.

When he opened his eyes, Carlo was kneeling in front of him, staring straight at him.

"You got a clock ticking on you, Frankie boy?"

Frank sighed, hanging his head, even though it made him feel like he wanted to puke.

"We all got a clock, Carlo. You're the one who told me that, remember? If anything, mine is ticking too slow. I've been planning to speed it up."

He paused, waiting for Carlo to yell at him or, worse, to jump to his feet and insist they go find a psychiatrist immediately. But he didn't.

He just continued to look at him, an expression of solemn acceptance on his face.

"That what you're doing at Coney Island? Looking for a high place to jump off?"

"Nah, too big a mess," Frank said, completely seriously. "Can't have my girls look at that." Again, he paused, waiting for Carlo to say something. When he didn't, he shrugged his shoulders. "I just wanted one last day to remember the good times, you know? Try to feel like something other than a sad old man. Just for a little while."

Clasping one of Frank's hands in both of his, Carlo said softly, "That's exactly how I'd do it too. When we get to the end of the day… you want help? With finishing it off?"

Frank shook his head. "You don't need to do that."

"Hey, I'm not offering. And like I said, none of us *has to* do anything. Anyway, this is your deal. But like you said, no need to leave a mess. I can help you with that. If you want."

Frank looked down at the bottle of pills, now resting beside him on the bench. "I don't think that's enough to do the job. So yeah, if you could get more that might be a good option."

Carlo nodded. "You feeling all right now?"

"Better. When you chew 'em, the pills kick in quick."

"Good." With a mighty heave, Carlo pulled Frank to his feet, holding onto his wrists until he was sure he was steady on his feet. "Because we've still got a day of fun and adventure to have."

With a smile, Frank nodded and let Carlo lead him into the aquarium where, as promised, the first stop was to watch the seals, which Frank loved.

When he'd come here with the girls, it was always about the penguins. Why the penguins in particular, he never understood. For Frank, it was all about the seals. They were fun and seemed perpetually happy. Now, sitting in the bleachers with Carlo and a gaggle of other onlookers as the cute animals clapped and did tricks, Frank found himself feeling happy too.

For a few moments, Frank found himself wondering how it was to be a sea, also asking himself why human beings always had to be such miserable bastards, never contented in life.

There was no answer to it though. *It was as it was,* something else Carlo would have said.

CHAPTER 11

After the seals, Frank and Carlo took a lap through the aquarium, looking at the fish, the sharks, and really just the sheer beauty of it all. They'd done a lot with the place since he'd been there last and he hoped—whenever his girls had kids of their own—they'd bring them here at least once, even though it was a longer trip. And he also hoped that when they came here, they would tell their own children all about how they used to come here with Grandpa, all those years ago.

"You need to take a break, Frankie?" Carlo asked as they headed for the exit.

"Nah, the pills are kicking in good," Frank said, meaning every word of it. The pills didn't last for terribly long, but while they worked, they worked good.

While they'd been in the aquarium, Carlo had removed his jacket, showing off his shiny lavender collared shirt while they viewed the exhibits. He was always a snazzy dresser.

Now outside again, he stopped up short to put the jacket back on once they'd cleared the exit,

"Hey buddy, could you move please?" came a complaint from behind them. It was hardly aggressive, but no one dared ask 'big' Carlo to stand aside. Not if they knew him, anyway.

Frank whipped around to see a young man in his thirties with red hair just barely avoid colliding into Carlo's back. The redhead pivoted on his toes, weaving around Carlo and Frank like some kind of drugged-up ballet dancer, holding the massive cup of soda in his hand high above their heads, making sure not to spill any of it.

"How about you watch your mouth?" shot back Carlo, waving his hand at the guy in a classically Italian way.

The younger guy didn't slow his pace as he walked away, but yelled over his shoulder, "How about you do something with your time other than watching Goodfellas, you boomer fuck?"

"Get the hell out of here!" Carlo hollered at his back. The man had been much bigger than Carlo, but there was one thing to know about the Italian, and this was that his attitude made him a giant. There was no man or group of men who'd intimidate him.

"Give it a rest, Carlo," muttered Frank, not even annoyed at the young man. Carlo would have been a hell of a lot madder if the guy had run into him, spilling his coke all over what looked to be a five-thousand-dollar suit. He had watched the boy being careful with the soda.

"No respect! What is it with these Irish pricks, huh?"

"I'm fucking Mexican!" the redheaded man yelled from a distance.

Carlo gasped. "A redheaded Mex—what the hell is going on in the world, Frank?"

As mad as Carlo was at that guy's attitude, Frank burst out laughing. "You can't just tell by looking at people anymore. The neighborhoods stopped being so rigid. And plus, new people come in all the time. And they copy one another."

"Yeah. Doesn't seem to make people any nicer, though, does it?" He stared at the retreating man. "You want me to bring him back so you can kick his ass? You know, one last hurrah?"

"Carlo, even if you held him down the whole time, I'd probably still end up being the one lying on the floor in a bloody heap."

"Ah well, worth a shot. Thought he could just get a good punch in, you'd just drop down dead, and then he'd be mortified. 'What have I done?'" he mock cried, reaching for the sky.

"You sicko," Frank wheezed as he laughed, holding onto the wall for support.

"Yeah, I am. Of course, there's no guarantee he'd feel bad at all. The way people are these days. Probably wouldn't even stick around after stomping on your brain; wouldn't bother to see if you ever breathed again."

"Charming," said Frank, but what was spiraling in his head was, *ain't that the truth?*

It was exactly as Carlo said. People had gotten so callous, and it all made him sick to watch. That guy seemed like a normal person. But going into the city these days was like signing up for abuse. Annabella blamed it all on Covid. But Frank knew she was wrong about that.

She was just as naive now as he'd been as a kid. The lockdowns and the paranoia just served to bring what was already there, all that latent crap, bubbling to the surface. That was all.

"You're right about that. It breaks my heart, honestly," Frank said, reflecting on how almost everyone stepped over him as he'd been having two separate seizures, confirming what he'd been feeling for a long time. He couldn't put his finger on what had gone so wrong.

New York had been a pretty nasty place in the seventies already, but even then, there had always been that neighborhood camaraderie, that sense of everyone being in it together—whatever 'it' was. But for example, everyone hated the government and they were one in their hatred of it. And everyone hated the people from other neighborhoods, and everyone hated the immigrants who they felt were beginning to take over certain areas.

But something they all agreed on was how you took care of your own people.

Nowadays, people didn't even do that. They didn't do the bare minimum. Because actually, no one gave a shit about anyone else anymore, and they didn't even have the decency to pretend that they did. They barely even cared for their own relatives.

These folks didn't realize quite what it was they were missing out on, and that was at least half of the problem with modern-day society in New York. Having people in the neighborhood who knew you and looked out for you could literally save your life. Or at least your face. But they hadn't known it and lived it, and what you hadn't experienced, you could hardly miss.

But camaraderie had saved Frank on more than one occasion, specifically with Carlo.

It wasn't any mystery to him why people were leaving New York. It had always been a rough-and-tumble city full of rats and neighborhoods best avoided. But there had also been a sense of pride, a nationwide understanding that being a New Yorker meant something.

Well, it still did mean something, there was no denying it.

Today, it meant you were a delusional idiot with more money than brain capacity, quietly paying higher taxes than you should, all for the daily possibility of getting kicked onto the subway tracks by a lunatic who shoulda been put in jail years ago.

And on top of that, the filthy air quality wasn't getting any better. Every day in this place, you were lucky if the hoodlums didn't get you or the air choke you to death.

Frank swallowed back a loud laugh as best he could, making Carlo turn and stare, laughing too though he had no idea what had set Frank off.

It just seemed ironic that today of all days, the one on which Frank would gladly have been choked by the toxin-laden air, the atmosphere was somehow better than it had been for months.

Fastening the last jacket button, Carlo shook his shoulders back. "Some neighborhoods still get it. Especially those Dominicans. They're like us Italians used to be in our day. Good people. All good people, that's all. And there aren't many about." He squinted up at the sun, now starting its descent. "Listen, you want to go to the pier before it gets dark? It's a nice day."

Frank looked down at his own suit and dress shoes. Then at Carlo's.

"Not really dressed for the water. Wish I'd brought my flip flops."

"Oh, come on. You only live once. Hopefully!" He eyed Frank. "Look, we can buy some there. You know they got all those shops with tacky clothes."

He slapped Frank on the shoulder, prompting him to get moving.

It wasn't lost on Frank how intent Carlo was on keeping him moving, keeping him stepping forward, on to the next thing and the next, and then the one after that as if he was holding Frank back but without the need to say so. Maybe he just hoped Frank would value their good day out.

It just seemed he didn't want to give Frank any opportunity to say, 'It's time.'

Well, why not? The shore sounded good anyway.

He needed to look at something beautiful, something that reminded him that there was a universe bigger and greater than him, something beyond the pettiness of human cruelty. And what was more likely to do that than the chance to stare at a vast sea and a wide sky, its horizon off in the infinity? Only a trip to outer space could top it, something even Carlo couldn't arrange.

"We can get ourselves one of those pedal boats if you want," ventured Carlo, his eyes twinkling. "Used to love those things as kids, didn't we? Call it a regression therapy trip."

Frank snorted. "That's where your memory's letting you down. Regression, my ass. I actually couldn't stand those things when we were kids, so if you floated off with someone who was enjoying it, then it wasn't me. I got seasick. Now… I don't think I'd have the cardio strength."

"Yeah, and I probably couldn't fit in the seat," Carlo said and laughed, patting his humongous wobbling gut as they walked away from the aquarium. "Ah well. Was just an idea."

***

An hour later, with their bellies full of hot dogs with mustard and onions, plus a Coke, Carlo and Frank stood on the pier looking out onto the blue-green water. There were several others on the pier, also admiring the view, but they were mostly adults and had the sense to keep a safe distance between the different parties. So, at the very edge of it, Carlo and Frank were standing alone, enjoying the breeze and admiring the boats. The wind whipped up their thinning hair.

Once they'd eaten, there hadn't been much conversation, just a comfortable silence passing between two old buddies who no longer felt any need to fill every gap in their discussions.

They had just continued walking at a leisurely pace, stopping to rest when needed, all the way to the best view on Earth. At least as far as two Brooklyn boys were concerned.

"You believe in God still, Frankie?" Carlo asked, breaking the long silence at last.

Oddly enough, he'd been expecting the question. There was something about being around people who had known you when you were a kid that tended to make them more reflective. And with Frank planning his exit, it seemed Carlo had been a little deeper in thought than usual.

"Of course," he said, not mentioning his trip to Our Lady of Solace that morning.

"What do you mean of course?"

"I can't look at the wonder just on this planet and think it all sprang up by accident. Besides, Bianca felt God like he was a visiting uncle. As real as you standing here with me. So, as far as I'm concerned, even if I wasn't raised in the Church, God's real. And so is heaven. But I'm not as sure as she was about what it will be like. Or who gets in." He swallowed hard. "I'm not sure I believe that just being in the right church is enough to get you in."

Carlo nodded. "Yeah, we all went to the same catechism class. But I never bought into it. Especially with the last rites. You're telling me with the life I lived, all I need to do is say confession, take communion, and it's all wiped clean? Don't buy it. Seems like even in the afterlife, there's a toll in the hole. But hey, what do I know?"

Frank nodded, wishing he still had his drink, or a cigarette or something to do with his hands. Normally, when someone expressed a concern they wouldn't get into heaven, the right thing to do was generally to assure them they would. But with Carlo, Frank wasn't sure about that at all.

Of course, he wasn't sure about his own destination either. The Catholic Church was pretty clear on what you needed to do to get into those pearly gates. The thing that the Protestants got wrong, at least the ones Frank had heard talking on TV, was their idea that God's promises of reward were about Earth. He could never get behind the idea that material things like money were signs of God's favor. Any guy who ever met a miserable rich bastard knew that wasn't true.

But those sheisters in their fancy suits and Rolexes had to justify their materialism somehow. They couldn't very well tell their congregation to keep giving them money because Daddy needed gator boots. So instead of admitting they were vain and greedy, those megachurch pastors just said they were displaying God's favor with thousand-dollar sneakers and sprawling homes.

Frank didn't buy it, even if it seemed a lot of other people did, those who continued giving.

Life on Earth was temporary, but heaven was the destination, the place where there would be no more suffering. Just the reward of a life well-lived.

"You know, my youngest is into all that hippie crap. The new age mindfulness crowd," said Carlo, leaning back against the railing and crossing his arms. "Know what he says? All humans are just energy and what survives after your body dies has no memory of your life here on Earth. You believe that?"

"Nope. And I never will," said Frank, not missing a beat. What happened down here on Earth mattered and it dictated what would happen in the afterlife. He couldn't be convinced otherwise.

"At least I know Bianca is in heaven. That I know with certainty. My parents too. They had their flaws, but they took religion seriously. That's why I don't pray for them. Not that they'll get into heaven, I mean. Because I know they're already there. Couldn't be anywhere else."

Carlo nodded. "Love your neighbor as you love yourself. She always did that. I was always jealous of you,

Frank. Really, I mean that. Having a good woman like her. None of mine were ever good. Not one. Or maybe they were. But they weren't good with me."

Carlo's voice went slightly hoarse, and his sentence faded out; he looked down at his shoes.

Frank wished he could say something—anything—nice about a single one of the Mrs. Sanguinettis who had come and gone. But Maria, the first one, had been the only one he'd met. And she was a nasty piece of work, with adults anyway. In her defense, from what Frank saw, she doted on her sons. But after having Carlo and Maria over for dinner one night, Bianca had asked if they could please never come to the house again. And Frank had agreed immediately.

Bianca wasn't perfect but she was good in a way most other people weren't. Frank was nice to homeless people and other unfortunates—like kids with developmental issues—because he felt sorry for them. The general public felt inclined to be nice to the unfortunate and their families just out of a selfish relief that their own kids didn't get hooked on smack and end up on the streets, or that they didn't have schizophrenia.

Or they didn't have a child or a sibling born with an extra chromosome. Most people were kind to those types of people as penance for thinking, *Thank God it's them and not me.*

But Bianca wasn't that way. And she didn't teach the girls to be that way either. She could see the light of God in people, no matter who it was. And even though he loved it about her, if Frank was honest, it always made him feel pretty sick with himself.

Because if Bianca hadn't had that superhuman ability to love, she would have kicked his sorry ass to the curb a long time ago. And she would have been right to.

Maybe that was why he'd never judged Carlo for the life he lived. He never even got mad when Carlo would call him at his job and ask him to do 'favors' every now and again. He didn't really see himself as different from Carlo. Because even though he wasn't a gangster and had never killed anyone, that didn't make Frank a good person. And he knew it.

"Listen, Frankie, I know Bianca never liked me. You don't need to feel bad about it. I understood. Hell, even my own wives never liked me much. I can't blame a good girl like that for not wanting me around."

Frank looked up, meeting Carlo's eyes.

No, he hadn't forgotten about their falling out all those years ago. He hadn't forgotten about Frank telling him that no, he wouldn't add a beneficiary's name to a recently deceased client's life insurance policy after the fact. And as a matter of fact, Carlo should never call him again.

Of course, he hadn't said that Bianca knew what he was doing and demanded he put a stop to it. But it seemed Carlo just knew. And from the look in his eyes, he wasn't angry. He was ashamed. And it seemed he had been for a long time.

And so was Frank. He'd been so invested in being a big shot that he'd fixed more than a few pieces of paperwork on Carlo's behalf. And if Bianca hadn't put her foot down, he wasn't even sure he would ever have stopped.

Shameful. Both of them had lived shameful lives. Just in different ways.

They both returned their gazes to the water, each silently staring in opposite directions.

His heart aching, Frank tried to refocus on the water, letting the rhythm of the darkening waves mesmerize him. He wasn't paying attention to anything else around him.

Not Carlo standing solemnly beside him, the people walking behind him on the shore, and not the small vessels on the water.

But the sudden revving of a boat engine snapped his head up.

His eyes grew wide at the sight of a small tour ship coming in hot, moving way too fast for being this close to shore, barreling right toward the pier.

"Shit, Carlo, move!"

Even though Frank had set out to die this night, he had no intention for Carlo to join him. At the last minute before the boat reached the pier, his reflexes took over and he grabbed the well-built man by his expensive jacket and yanked him hard, driving them both backward, stumbling out of the way of the ship… and into the icy water.

Everything seemed to crash in all around him, muffling the sound of the ship's hull crunching against the wooden pylons of the pier and the metallic walkway. Frank thrashed around in the water, fighting against Carlo's bulk pressing against him, driving him down.

Every nerve fired and his head was screaming at him, *get out, get out, get out!* The shock of the water's coldness horrified him as he fought to avoid gasping in a breath, still underwater.

No. Let go. Let go now. It's perfect. It's everything you want.

Frank closed his eyes as he released his hold on Carlo, pushing away from him and trying to muster up the courage to open his mouth and take in a breath.

Now was the time.

Before he could do it, hands grabbed him around the collar and, with a strength and speed Frank had difficulty understanding, pulled him to the surface, shoving his head clear of the water with an almighty gasp.

"You all right, Frank?" Carlo asked, giving him another shake. "I know this water's probably full of piss and dead bodies, but I mean besides that?"

Rivulets of freezing water dripped down his face as he nodded, marveling at how Carlo seemed to be floating on his own, without even treading water.

I guess that gut has its benefits, like an in-built lifejacket.

Fighting against the water and his own body, Frank brought himself back to the wreckage of the pier, where he and Carlo slowly crawled onto the shore beside the wreckage of the boat, both of their limbs clumsy from the cold and from being wrapped in the soaking fabric of their suits.

What had that maniac boat pilot been thinking?

"Hey asshole!" he called or tried to. His voice was hoarse and barely above a whisper as he looked at the boat, motionless and wedged against the ruptured shoreline, its engine steaming.

"You think the guy was drunk?" Carlo asked, kicking off his shoes and socks, then pulling off his jacket, which collapsed onto the sand with a wet thud.

"I don't know," Frank said, likewise pulling off his jacket. It was only making him colder. He didn't see anyone climbing out of the boat. Had it even been occupied? Maybe it was and all the passengers were dead? Did the captain have a medical emergency, and that's why he'd crashed?

As Frank wrapped his arms around his body, trying in vain to get warm, he turned to look back at the water, trying not to be angry at Carlo for pulling him out. For saving him.

Seeming to read his mind, Carlo took hold of his elbow, helping him navigate the sandy ground as they moved away from the water.

"Not yet, Frankie. The day ain't over yet. You don't get away that easy."

CHAPTER 12

The thing about fear was that you could never predict how it would affect you. The world was full of people talking in bars or over the dinner table about some local tragedy like a mass shooting or a natural disaster, and they wanted everyone in hearing distance to know that if they had been there at the time, things would have gone a lot different.

Those people who ran from the mass shooter, leaving a disabled person to fend for themselves? That wouldn't have happened if *this guy* had been there. Those poor people who'd died of thirst because rescue workers couldn't get to them in the rubble in time?

That wouldn't have happened if *this guy* had been there to help. It was human nature for a person to overestimate their abilities and bravery in any given situation.

Frank didn't dare to judge people for it, but he respected the ones who had somehow grown sufficiently self-aware enough to know that what they thought they'd do in a situation and what they actually ended up doing could well be very different, poles apart, in fact.

Frank, and all other actuaries, were particularly susceptible to this kind of overestimation of their own excellence. In the insurance business, it was common to see all kinds of tragedy, and in Frank's role and similar roles, they assessed it for its cause. Had the tragedy been preventable? If so, who could have prevented it? Was the claimant at fault or was it someone else's negligence?

Having that kind of distance and the luxury of perspective in which to assess a situation created the false idea that if you were only careful enough and meticulous enough, you could avoid just about anything. Oh, you don't want to develop cancer? Just eat right and exercise. And don't smoke or dip, for God's sake. You don't want to get in a car wreck? That's fine. Just drive carefully and stick to daylight hours. You might not go your whole life without a wreck, but you're more likely to only suffer fender benders. Especially if you wear your seatbelt.

An insurance man all his life, Frank almost couldn't help himself from calculating the damages for which that asshole who'd driven the boat into the pier could be liable.

You got one hell of a lawsuit on your hands, buddy. Hope you lawyer up.

Even soaking wet, cold, and now covered with sand, which might be the worst sensation in the world, still those numbers kept ticking through Frank's head as he and Carlo joined the rest of the crowd forming around the accident site.

Depending on how many people had been on the boat, that could culminate in a class action lawsuit. How badly had they each been hurt?

Frank hadn't sustained any injuries, but he had a case on his hands for pain and suffering if he wanted to be a claimant. Plus, the criminal charges of reckless endangerment. Possibly even depraved indifference manslaughter, depending on the circumstances.

The sound of sirens filled the air, getting louder as an ambulance and a couple police cars pulled up, parting the crowd like the Red Sea to let them through.

"That's some impressive reaction time," mused Carlo.

"Especially for New York," Frank agreed.

The strobing lights created a strange effect on the crowd.

Frank wondered, how did he and Carlo look to these people, the two of them standing in their soaking wet, sand-covered dress suits? It was likely the people around thought they were bums—well, maybe they thought Frank was one.

Carlo's suit, even in the state it was in, was clearly far too expensive for that. And tailored.

Frank looked down at himself.

Maybe he could admit to looking like a bum who had stolen someone else's suit.

"I'm freezing my ass off, Carlo. We need to go buy some cheap Bermuda shorts or something before I freeze to death."

"Yeah, you're right about that. Even my fat ass is cold," Carlo agreed, taking him by the elbow as they navigated away from the crowd. They side stepped the gathered men, women, and children as best as they could, not wanting to rub water and sand-covered clothing on anyone.

Just as they made their way to the edge of the crowd, Frank saw a flash of a woman's hair—pulled up in a twist, the same way Bianca used to. The blouse looked like one of hers as well.

"Bianca?" he yelled, quickening his pace, trying to weave his way through the people at the edges of the crowd. Could it be her?

"Hey Frank, where you going? The stores are the other way!"

Ignoring him, Frank walked as fast as he could, his wet feet rubbing painfully inside his waterlogged shoes. He had heard stories that people who were dying saw visions of their loved ones. Was he catching hypothermia? Had she come to collect him and take him to heaven?

Breaking free of the crowd, he whipped his head around, scanning every face, seeking her out. But she was gone.

"Hey, you having another attack or something?" Carlo caught up with him, jerking him around to face him.

"No," he said, swatting away Carlo's hand. "I just thought I saw…"

He trailed off, embarrassed to say it out loud.

But Carlo had obviously heard him yell out for her, so he nodded. "All right, here's what we're gonna do. Ya listening?" He tapped Frank's chin to bring his eyes back up, then continued. "We're gonna go buy some ugly ass tourist clothes so we ain't walking around like some wet fish. Then I'm gonna take you to my guy and get you something nice to wear. Something classy. Sound good?"

Frank sighed. "I won't be around when the suit's done."

"Hey, I'm not talking nothing bespoke. I don't like you that much, Frankie." Carlo laughed, slapping him on the shoulder. "If you want me to drop that kind of money on you, you'd have to grow some nice melons."

He laughed again as he held his hands up in front of him in a cupping gesture.

Frank burst out laughing, following him onto the sidewalk.

"You're a real sicko, you know that?"

Even with the crowd from the wreck, they were able to navigate to the nearest souvenir shop. Lucky for them, it was a well-stocked store, and extremely clean, honestly pretty rare throughout New York. But one look at the guy behind the counter made it all clear. He was an older guy, South Asian, who wore a short-sleeved collared shirt, with every single button done up. His pants were starched and pressed, and he even had creases in his sleeves.

This guy communicated stern efficiency. A man after Frank's own heart.

After looking through the racks for a while, he selected a souvenir long-sleeved t-shirt and cheap cargo pants from the racks, picking out the ones that had the thickest and best material. For good measure, he got the cheapest sneakers they sold there and a pack of socks.

Everything he wore was soaking wet. His only regret was that they didn't sell boxers here. Though he could do without, he supposed.

Carlo picked out something similar, only in larger sizes.

"I got this one," Frank said, holding up his hand as Carlo reached for his wallet. "No sense you buying me two outfits."

After paying with a debit card—he knew better than to bother the efficient shop owner with his soggy cash—the two of them took their new clothes into the restroom to change. As expected, the men's room was clean, spacious, and mercifully empty.

Taking up a spot in separate corners, they started the slow, uncomfortable work of stripping off their sodden pants, socks, and shoes, Frank holding onto the wall the whole time. He was still shaking from the cold, dreading having to unbutton his shirt. His hands were blue, toes purplish.

He'd have to get out of the wet gear as soon as possible and into something warm and dry, or hypothermia would claim him.

But before he could grasp the first shirt button, his body started shaking.

Now, it wasn't from the cold anymore.

Oh no…

Bracing his back against the wall, he sank to the floor, resisting his body as it spasmed and shook, trying to keep his head from slamming against the tiles on the wall.

"Ah shit!"

Carlo skidded across the tile floor, catching Frank by the elbows before he crashed his tailbone into the floor.

Luckily, it wasn't a full-blown seizure this time, but the tremors took hold of his body, and he could do nothing but sit and shake, waiting for the spell to pass and trying not to swallow his tongue. They were violent shakes to be experiencing on hard tiles, something like rigors. Even so, he already knew how much worse the seizures could get.

Having his bare ass against the bathroom floor for the entire shaking spell was hardly pleasant, but there was a small blessing; no one else came into the bathroom.

Were these symptoms an effect of withdrawals?

He had seen on the internet that seizures could occur if you stopped medications suddenly. Maybe this was just a lower grade of what he'd experienced earlier in the day.

He sucked in a deep breath, holding his neck as still as possible while he shook, oddly grateful to find himself still conscious and with some modicum of control over himself. Though if a man had to piss himself, the men's room was the place to do it.

"It's all right Frankie, you get it all out. But don't kick the bucket now, okay? They'll think you're a junkie if you kick it in a boardwalk men's room. Just sayin'," Carlo said, the light tone in his voice belied by his clenched teeth.

The shaking stopped suddenly, rather than petering out as his previous episodes had. Still exhausted, he sighed, letting Carlo lean him back against the wall.

"You need another pill, Frankie?" he asked.

Frank nodded, woefully looking over at his wet trousers crumpled a few feet away.

Carlo butt-scooted over to the pants and, rifling through the pockets, came up empty. "Looks like they didn't make it out of the water."

"Crap."

"Not a big deal, honestly," Carlo said. "I got a guy. Well, he's not *my* guy. The family don't go in for the drugs, you know that. But I know where he works. We'll go as soon as we're done here. You need help getting dressed?"

"If I needed another guy putting on my boxers for me, I'd just as soon you brain me with the edge of the sink, and we'd be done with it."

"Duly noted," he said and laughed, scooting away, and leaving Frank to get dressed.

Mercifully free of the tremors, though sore now from the prolonged effort of it, Frank pulled his wet shirt over his head, knowing better than to fool with the buttons. Staying seated on the floor, he carefully put on his new clothes, using the paper towels in the restroom to remove any lingering wetness on his skin. At least there actually were paper towels instead of those horrible air blower things. Frank hated those.

After dressing, he took a few more minutes to catch his breath, but using the wall once again, he was able to get to his feet and leave the men's room. His wet suit and shoes were staying right where they'd been left, crumpled in a wad under one of the sinks. Normally, he would have shoved it all into one of the trash cans to avoid leaving the mess. But he didn't trust himself to bend over and retrieve them. And he didn't want to ask Carlo to do it, as he too had left his old clothes on the floor. He only hoped the shop owner wouldn't be too put out.

They both nodded at the man behind the counter as they walked out of the shop, taking note of the slight smile on his face.

"Maybe we're not the first ones to come in here for new clothes," he wondered aloud as they walked outside.

"With the number of drunk assholes in and out of here every day?" Carlo said, "I guarantee you that guy makes bank selling new pants to guys who puked or pissed on themselves."

They both had a good laugh, first at the idea of the drunken idiots, and then at themselves as they walked past a full-length mirror nailed to the side of one of the buildings.

"Oh, holy hell, look at that mess," Carlo guffawed, turning away from his reflection.

"We're sporting 'the Dad look' as Daniella would say. You know she actually threw out my sneakers once because she said they were 'dad shoes'?"

Carlo laughed all the harder. "That's one good thing about having boys. They don't get wrapped up in that crap." He let out a few more laughs, then took a deep breath as he straightened. "All right, Frankie. Let's go get you some pills."

Frank only nodded, but he had to restrain himself from sighing in relief.

The time between needing another dose was getting shorter and if he didn't get a pill soon, maybe he wouldn't make it to the end of the day. And for some weird reason, he wasn't ready to check out. Not yet. He'd been having too much fun for a change.

And besides, his last moment on Earth would be Carlo yelling at him for crapping out early.

Chapter 13

Frank hadn't known exactly what to expect when Carlo led him away from Coney Island in search of the drug dealer. Maybe some fresh-faced wisecrack kid wearing a puffy jacket.

What he was not expecting to see as they rounded the corner was a towering, big-bellied Dominican with a beard that would put Captain Sinbad to shame. At the sight of the gargantuan man, Frank hung back, his eyes widening at the sight of him.

The feeling was seemingly mutual.

The big man's eyes stretched wide when he caught sight of Frank and Carlo, and he dropped everything in his hands and took off running.

"Damn it," seethed Carlo, lobbing the heavy thermal tumbler he'd purchased at the souvenir shop right at the retreating man.

Carlo had always had a cannon for an arm and obviously, age hadn't taken it from him because the heavy Thermos nailed the man right between his shoulder blades with a loud *ting!*

He tumbled forward, landing face-first on the pavement, and the other men to whom he'd been talking scattered like roaches.

"I thought you said he was a friend?" Frank asked, out of breath from the excitement of it.

"I never said that," Carlo retorted.

Even with the ugly tee shirt and Bermuda shorts, Carlo cut an imposing figure as he marched up to the man on the pavement, who by now had rolled over onto his back.

"Hey man, I did what you said! If someone rocked up on one of your people, it wasn't me this time, I swear!"

The man splayed his hands in front of his face, obviously expecting a beating.

What the hell is this all about?

"Nah, you learned your lesson last time, didn't you, Miguel? Anyway, I like a man who can take his licks," Carlo said, taking a knee in front of him. "Look, I'm not here to play rough. I just need some Oxy for my friend here. I need a lot of it and I'll pay fair market for it. Sound good?"

Miguel blinked rapidly, his mouth hanging slightly open in confusion. The way he kept his hands up made Frank wonder if Miguel thought this might be a trick, a ruse to catch him out.

Carlo didn't say anything else, just waited patiently, at least until his knees started hurting. After a minute of shocked silence, Carlo stood up again. Then he looked down in an exasperated fashion. "Do I need to go talk to your runner myself?"

"No!" shouted Miguel, then pressed his lips together, taking a breath to correct his tone. "I- uh, I'll be happy to get that for you. How much you need?"

"Enough for a heavy user to make an exit plan, if you know what I'm saying."

There was that face again, Miguel looking like a man who was certain he was being tricked as he propped himself up on his elbows.

"Hey man, I just help people have a good time…"

"I'm sure you can see I'm not one of your regular junkies," Frank said quietly. He hadn't intended for Carlo to just come out and say what he just had said, but there was no reason for this stranger to feel bad about anything. "I got a condition. And it won't get better. Ever," he said.

Something resembling understanding flashed over Miguel's face, and he gave a slight nod. "All right. It'll be five hundred flat," he said, getting to his feet.

Carlo pursed his lips and raised an eyebrow.

"That's a friend price, I swear. Inflation hits us too," Miguel said, holding up his hands, this time in resignation.

With a low huff, Carlo pulled out his wallet, which was still soggy, and withdrew five C notes, all of which were moist but not too bad. He'd gone to the ATM before they left the boardwalk, as all the cash that he'd taken into the water would be unusable for a while.

As a sign of respect, Miguel took it without counting, then turned and walked back towards where he'd been hanging out before.

"What was that all about?" Frank watched the man for any sign he'd take off running again.

Carlo laughed. "A couple years back, I was having dinner and that Dominican nobody just sat down at my table, introduced himself, and said he had a business proposal for the family. That we were on the decline, and he could help."

Frank felt his mouth drop open. Shaking his head in disbelief, he gasped out, "Wait... he came up to you with a business arrangement *without* being introduced?"

Carlo nodded, eyes wide in shock, even after all these years. "Yeah. You believe that shit? If he'd been a kid, I'd understand. They don't know nothing. But him. He's been in the game for a long time. So, we kicked the shit out of him. Good and proper, you know what I'm saying? Dude was probably eating through a tube for a while."

Frank blanched. "But he's still breathing."

"Hey, I'm a nice guy. Everyone says. I went easy on him. What can I say?"

Frank laughed, even though it wasn't really funny. But the idea that any New Yorker, no matter the ethnicity, would approach a known wise guy without being introduced was insane. There was a whole protocol around it. Usually, another made man, or an associate of the family, would make an introduction. When the introduction was made, the one introducing the two parties knew he was taking responsibility for the new unknown. If that new unknown made a mistake or did a bad deal for the made man, the introducer would be liable.

Everyone knew that, thanks to the movies.

Because of *Donnie Brasco* and *The Sopranos*, some guy in Oregon right now could recite the rules about doing business with the mob. So even though Miguel's ass-whoopin' was severe, Frank thought maybe he'd deserved it a little.

Coming back from around the corner, Miguel shook a bottle of pills, so they could hear it was full. He then tossed it at Carlo, who caught it easily.

"Do I need to count these?" he asked.

"You can. But you don't need to," said Miguel, trying to look unconcerned, but failing.

Satisfied, Carlo handed them to Frank, who immediately took the cap off and popped one of the pills into his mouth, gagging as he ground it between his teeth.

Miguel gave one last nod to Carlo as if to ask, *are we good?*

Carlo looked to Frank. And Frank nodded; this was the right stuff. Tasted suitably vile, but already, he could feel it beginning to work its way through his veins.

When Miguel received a nod in return from Carlo, he turned and walked—briskly—away.

Frank sighed, reveling in the warmth of the pills moving through his system. Miguel had given him the real deal, and it was wonderful stuff when you were feeling this shit.

Carlo jerked his head. "Alrighty, it can't wait any longer. Let's go see my guy for a suit."

***

When Carlo had promised to take Frank to 'his guy' to get a suit, he wasn't expecting to be taken to Elias Baumann, the man who made suits for governors, presidents… and rap moguls.

"Honestly, Mr. Sanguinetti, you do this as a joke, yes?" the rail-thin bleached blond man asked, his Swiss accent growing thicker as he pursed his lips in disapproval. "It is not Halloween. There is other holiday devoted to the grotesque?"

Carlo threw his head back and laughed, nudging Frank through the door of the shop. "What's a matter, Elia? You don't like Bermuda shorts?"

From the look on his face, it was clear the upper-crust tailor didn't like shorts at all, but he seemed to like Carlo, or at least respected his money. The hours of his shop were emblazoned on the glass door, indicating he should have closed at 4 p.m. But here it was, inching toward six o'clock, and he had let them in with no issue.

Likewise, Elias didn't seem too happy at proffering something off the rack.

"Mr. Sanguinetti, I have something in the back to your measurements. This, no problem. But your friend…" He let his eyes drift up and down Frank as if he were a slab of spoiled meat. "It will be basic, the suit I provide. It will not be to my standard. You are not a client, sir? I do not remember your face if you are."

"No," Frank rasped out. "I've never been here."

And it was true. Frank had never been to Elias Baumann's shop before. But he had owned one of his very expensive shirts.

It was the shirt that had very nearly cost him everything. And he wasn't at all happy to be here. He'd been so sure Bianca wouldn't notice the luxury shirt hanging in his closet.

Because in his myopic view, clothes were clothes, and there was nothing personal or unique about them. But of course, that wasn't true. Not true at all, and a discerning eye could see the difference, the many ways in which that shirt exuded superiority over the rest. Another woman had bought that shirt for him. And he'd brought it into his wife's house.

"Come with me, sir. I will bring you several options and we will find the one that works best. On your account, Mr. Sanguinetti?" Elia asked, gesturing to Frank to follow him.

"That's right. I want him to look like a million bucks, Elia. I have faith in you."

"I try, but I cannot guarantee, sir, not for your guest. I speak the truth; I have to work with what I have and limited time, you understand? I guarantee only he will look better than he does now," Elias said, keeping a crisp pace to the fitting room while Frank trudged behind.

"You all right, Frankie boy?" Carlo asked, lowering his voice.

He nodded back at him, relieved to disappear out of sight into the dressing rooms.

The infamous shirt incident had come around the same time as he'd cut ties with Carlo all those years ago. He had been forty-five at the time, making money hand over fist at work. Daniella had been a toddler, Viviana in elementary school, and Annabella had just moved up to middle school. Frank was in the prime mid-life crisis demographic and boy, did he lean into it.

He had recently gotten a new job at Turner Actuarial, contracting with the biggest insurance firms in the game, not to mention other industries such as the credit bureaus.

Previously, he had never been one to define himself by his job or his salary; he'd been content just to be seen as a family man. But somehow, this was different.

Maybe he'd long since believed he'd never get a chance to work for one of those Manhattan firms, and so he wasn't prepared for the ego boost he got when it happened for him.

It was much harder work than he'd ever had to put in before, but he'd made it. Though making it was one thing, and proving himself and deserving it were something else. So, he used to sleep at the office sometimes to avoid the daily commute and get in more hours, something Bianca never got used to. She had never been a passive-aggressive woman, always outspoken and unafraid to voice what she was thinking, whatever it happened to be that dogged her mind. This was something Frank had normally appreciated.

But in this case, he would get angry and defensive with her.

"This is what it means to work at a top firm! This is New York, not podunk town, USA!" he'd sneered at her over dinner.

"Frank, we moved *out* of New York to have a family."

"And we do have a family, and in case you haven't noticed, I'm providing for that family by working long hours. And I wish you appreciated that. But I guess it's too much to expect."

As promised, Elias brought Frank several suits—navy, tan, chocolate brown, and cobalt. No black though. "Black is for business and funerals, sir. I won't have it," Elias snipped.

Funny… *she* had told him that too.

The rift between him and Bianca had begun even before she'd ever got hired at his firm. And most of the problem came from him, directed at her. He hadn't fully seen the value in her then.

There came the disrespect, the dismissal of the way Bianca kept their house and looked after the children. All the traits and skills he had previously most valued in her became something trivial, unimportant, worthy of derision. Somehow, everything he had ever wanted in a woman changed, all with the act of getting a new job, one that made him feel too self-important.

Then *she* had got hired as Carlo's assistant.

Pretty, young, and for some reason, interested in Frank. *She* wanted his opinion and laughed at his jokes, making a point to bring him coffee whenever she made a run.

Looking back, it was easier to pretend that she'd targeted him. Oh, how he would have behaved so perfectly if only that loose woman hadn't set her sights on him. But of course, that hadn't been the case. *She'd* been friendly. *She'd* been flirty. But *he* was the one who had asked her out for cocktails. *He* was the one who had mentioned on a regular basis that he slept at the office, and if she worked too late, she might find she had to do so as well.

"Frank?" A gentle rap came on the door. "You okay?"

"Fine," he croaked out, realizing too late he had tears running down his face.

"Come on and let me in, why don't you?" Carlo whispered.

Frank obliged, wiping his face as Carlo came into the dressing room.

"Something hurt?"

Frank let out a sad laugh, plucking at the collar of the fine linen shirt he was trying on. "Just remembering the bad times. What a piece of shit I am."

Carlo sighed, reaching out and helping with the buttons on Frank's shirt. "You're not a piece a shit, Frank. Don't be stupid. You're the best—"

"You ever screw around on your wife?" he asked, cutting him off before he could give him a compliment he didn't deserve.

Without missing a beat, Carlo shot back, "I screwed around on all of them. Why you think I've been married so many times?"

"Well, mine didn't deserve it."

"Of course, she didn't. Mine didn't deserve it either, even though I told myself they did at the time. We all do it, you know. We're all prone to being stupid. Young and immature."

He finished the last of Frank's buttons and looked at him. "We always tell ourselves lies to justify our dirt. Bianca find out, did she?"

He nodded. "Yeah. She sure did."

It wasn't long after *she* started staying the night at the office periodically that she'd bought him the shirt in question, a noticeably fine bespoke linen shirt that went perfectly with quite a few of his overpriced suits. If there was one thing Frank never did, it was shop for clothing.

Not him. Never once. He would tell Bianca what he wanted, she would pick out a few options, and he would select his favorite. He was color blind, so it was better for everyone to have her do the leg work. And she did the family budget, making it that much more reasonable for her to select his clothing options. He'd never even considered fine tailoring and big brands.

So, when Bianca was putting his drycleaning away, of course she saw that shirt hanging in the closet, and knew immediately: it wasn't one she had bought. Not a chance of it.

She also knew he hadn't bought it for himself.

So, where had it come from all of a sudden?

Something inside of her must have known because her voice was shaking when she'd asked. Intuition, they call it—a woman's instinct to know if her man has been messing around.

Looking back, maybe Frank had left that wretched thing there in the closet for her to find intentionally, on a subconscious level. That was what people said at timesd, that men wanted to get found out even if they told themselves and their friends otherwise.

He was arrogant too, smug and obnoxious about it, almost challenging Bianca to find it. "She'll never tell the difference," he'd said aloud to himself, smoothing it over with his hand and hanging it in the closet. That stupid, shortsighted, utterly idiotic statement would have been ridiculous to anyone. Of course, she would know the difference. And she did. Right away.

That night, when he'd come home late as usual, there she was, Bianca sitting up waiting for him. She asked him to have a seat on their bed, and her voice was trembling. But still she asked calmly and without even raising her voice, "So, I suppose you'll want a divorce?"

It sent him reeling. She was way too clever for him and far too good at this. He knew immediately what the issue was, and his blood ran cold. His Bianca knew. What had he done?

But just like so many cheats, he would go through with this pointless façade.

"Of course not. Why would you ask that?" he demanded in a tone making it seem as if she had been the one to wound him.

"It's obvious why, isn't it? Because you have someone else. And it's serious enough for her to be buying you clothing. *Do* you want a divorce?" she pressed.

"I'm not—"

"I'm not having it, Frank!" She stood up and pointed her finger directly at his face. "You might think I'm just a glorified maid but I'm not stupid. That's one thing I am not. And if you continue this farce of denial, then *I* shall give you a divorce—whether you want one or not."

Her tone stopped his subterfuge and lies cold.

"Yes, as I say, if you want a divorce, then we'll get one," she said, her tone quiet but firm. "I shan't fight for you. Not now you're plainly disloyal to me. I would have to have no self-esteem to do that. So, think carefully. If you don't want to divorce, if you want to continue being married and a part of this family, then you will turn in your notice at work tomorrow. You will cut off contact with that woman, whoever she is. You will not go to see her at work, and you will not explain yourself to her. Understand? You will go to confession, and we will go to marital counseling with Father Donovan. And these are the sole conditions on which I will go forward."

"Bianca—"

"This isn't a negotiation," she interrupted, though still not raising her voice. He honestly didn't know how she kept herself so together. "You will do all these things, or I will leave. Then you can embarrass yourself as much as you want without embarrassing me and your daughters."

Bold, direct, unafraid. Italian women had a reputation for having tempers, for being overly emotional and fiery in their delivery. But he got none of those explosive outbursts with screaming and swearing that had been such a staple of his Italian neighborhood growing up.

Having Bianca speak to him like that, in such a direct, matter-of-fact way, was unexpected.

And it left him not knowing what to do. He was in a mess of his own making, and he was going to have to extricate himself before it was too late. And he'd be all alone in doing it.

Perhaps in having an affair like that, he had hoped to upset her, to make her feel less worthy so he could put her down and play mind games. Well, she was having none of it.

He feared he would lose this particular battle of wills and wits and felt thoroughly stupid. But he was not about to show that to Biance, now, was he?

"Well, damn," Carlo said, admiration clear in his voice. "I guess that's why you left Manhattan. And here I thought it was all because of me. And our... *arrangement.*"

Frank shook his head. "Nah. Bianca was done turning a blind eye. To everything. So, it was kind of a cascade effect. I'm sorry about that by the way," Frank said, pulling on one of the navy suits. "I hope I didn't cause problems with you and your... associates."

Carlo shrugged. "It wasn't a big problem. I wish I'd a handled it better to be honest. I wish we hadn't stopped talking. We were friends, and nothing should have spoiled that."

"Me too," Frank said. Though he wasn't sure he would have made the same decisions if he and Carlo had still been friends.

Friends were always important—another thing Bianca had taught him. The hard way.

Even as he'd stood in his marital bedroom, being confronted with his sin by his wife who had done nothing but love and support him, Frank had actually told her he needed to think about it, that he would give her an answer the next day. It was, he supposed, a way to say she had not won this battle quite yet. Though of course, deep down, he must have sensed he was already the loser.

He went to sleep on the couch that night, about to make the biggest mistake of his life. And he would have, he was sure of it, if for no other reason than out of pigheadedness.

He hated any woman telling him what to do and what decisions he must take. Even his wife could not do that to him, couldn't expect he would just obey like a scolded dog.

In fact, he would have walked away just to be bloody minded. If not for Muriel.

His wife's pain was not enough to shake him out of his testosterone and ego-fueled cruelty. But his wife's friend was, even though until that morning on the way to work, he had never so much as spoken to her before. She had been over to the house many times, and he had heard Bianca talk about her. But he'd never had a conversation with her himself. Never really gave her the time of day. Why would he? Whenever Muriel was around, he usually went to his study and simply left the women to talk about whatever it was women discussed when men were not there.

But his commute to Manhattan was a long one, involving a ferry and a train.

It seemed Muriel had a similar route, and it was at the train station that she'd spotted him, and now, she had something to say.

And exactly what she said was, "Hey shithead!" Oddly in New York, such an outburst wasn't particularly noteworthy, so Frank didn't turn around, though he heard the words clearly.

"Hey, Frank Vitale? Shithead! You! You don't hear me talking to you?"

That got his attention. He turned to see a refined woman in a business suit, a posh wool coat, and what looked like an expensive leather satchel; she came striding toward him, her black commuting sneakers perfectly matching her skirt and blazer.

"Muriel?" It took him a second to recognize her with the outright anger on her face, a far cry from the serene smile she normally wore when they briefly crossed paths in the kitchen at home.

"Yeah, it's Muriel. Funny how I've been to your house about fifty times and you still gotta squint at me. What the hell are you doing going to work? Your wife and the mother of your kids tells you to make a decision about the future of your family and you just sneak outta the house without giving her an answer? I pegged you for a dick, but didn't think you were a coward too."

The other commuters didn't stop or even slow, but Frank's face heated as more than one looked out the corner of their eye as they passed, trying to grab for themselves a snatch of the confrontation so they'd have some fun gossip to tell once they got to work.

Frank felt his pulse skyrocket with anger.

Bianca must have picked up the phone after he'd left the house. She just couldn't keep their private family business to herself, could she? She just had to go crying to Muriel. Who did she think she was blabbing about their personal business to her friends?

Maybe this kind of disloyalty was one reason why he'd been forced to be… um, disloyal.

He cringed. That didn't make any sense, did it? His Bianca had been faithful through and through, and it was hardly fair to blame her for his own failings. If she needed someone to talk to now, who could blame her? But he'd only wished it didn't have to be the fiery Muriel.

"I told her you were a disrespectful shit and that you didn't even deserve the warning," Muriel seethed, stepping closer to him, pointing her finger at his chest. "I told her to lawyer up and take you for everything you got. You know what she said to me? 'I love him too much, Muriel. How could I do that to him?' But you don't seem to have a problem doing this to *her,* do you? You know how ashamed she is? How crushed? How scared she is of being just another single mom who's gotta beg her ex for child support while he's off starting a new family?

"All she could say was 'he's different. He's not like that.' But you *are* like that, aren't you Frankie boy? You're *all* like that. Let me guess, you're eyeing a sports car too?

"You're a fucking cartoon character and you should be ashamed of yourself. You think the car and the hot young thing next to you will distract people from your receding hairline and your crows' feet? You're just a sad, middle-aged schlub who wants to spread the misery around.

"For once in your life, think of the wife who gave you everything and asked for nothing. Give her the divorce or get your shit together, you rat bastard. Or you'll have me to deal with."

Muriel hadn't waited for his response, had barely taken a breath between her words as she let him have it, her face twisting into one of outright disgust.

In all his life, including his rough, working-class childhood, no one had ever looked at Frank like that. As if he was shit on the bottom of someone's shoe.

Maybe it was the look more than the words that froze him in place, gluing him to the spot as he watched Muriel walk away and get on the train. He had stayed there for a long, long time, replaying every syllable Muriel had said to him in his head, over and over.

He hadn't even gotten on the train. He'd stayed on the platform, staring blankly into thin air, long after Muriel had gotten onto her train and the morning commute thinned to a trickle.

Of all people, it had been Muriel, Bianca's friend, rather than Bianca herself, to throw cold water on Frank, shocking him out of the stupid macho fantasies in which he'd been indulging. The effect was immediate, like an addict quitting cold turkey.

There, on that platform, Frank decided who he wanted to be and what he wanted. And there would be no waffling or half measures.

"But it got better, right?" Carlo asked now, holding out the chocolate brown suit for him to try on next. "You made it right. I knew you would, Frank."

"It's not really something you can ever make right. You know that. I mean yeah, I quit. I got rid of *her.* And I went to the priest with Bianca. But still, that stink don't wash off. We were never the same after that, and how could I expect us to be? She stopped all the small things she used to do for me. Not out of spite or anything, just because of the stink that hung about. She'd lost her respect for me, and she'd lost her desire. Just like that—gone in a heartbeat. I did believe she still loved me because why else would she have let me stay? But she couldn't get that trust back. Like I said, that stink don't wash away no matter what."

"Pretty sure it does, Frank. I think that's the whole thing about being a Christian. If you're sorry, and you atone, then it's washed away. Ain't that what we were taught? Not trying to get preachy on you but why punish yourself for something that you've been forgiven for?"

Sitting down on the bench, Frank sighed.

"Because of the look on her face, Carlo, that's why. When I came home and apologized, telling her I'd quit, she looked so hurt, but also surprised. She'd been expecting me to leave her that day because that's who I am. Who I was. The guy who betrayed the only one who really loved him. She'd begun preparing for… for a life without me. I could see it in her face."

"Ah, Frank," Carlo groaned as he lowered himself onto the bench beside Frank, barely able to squeeze in next to him. "The fact you're ashamed at all proves you're a good man.

She would've known it, Frank. Honestly, she would. There were a lot of things I done that would turn your stomach. And I slept like a baby afterwards. It wasn't until years later that I realized I done wrong. Too late, actually… But you, you saw it right away."

They looked at one another, saying in unison, "But only because of Muriel."

"But that doesn't matter, Frank," said Carlo. "You didn't leave your wife. Why doesn't matter. You see Frank, if that had been me… I would've screwed up, made a bad situation worse. But you, I've always known you're a good man. No doubt about—"

"Carlo, please." Frank raised a palm to say, *please don't say any more.*

Carlo trailed off, clamping his jaw shut and staring at the dressing room door.

"But it's not too late for you either," Frank said out of the blue since it wasn't even supposed to be about Carlo. Frank nudged his friend. *"You're* still here too. You can make it right. You have all the same opportunities as I did to make it right. You could do it today, Carlo."

"Nah. Some things you can't make right. But *you* did. You made it right in the moment. You made it up to your wife without fighting against the need to do it. And that's why you're a good man. And why I'm not."

Together, they sat silently in the dressing room, each reflecting on their failures. Frank knew better than to argue with Carlo over his self-assessment. He didn't know details, but it was clear where Carlo's money came from. And when they'd been young, Frank had pleaded with his friend to do something, *anything*, else for a living.

But he had gone into it anyway. He liked the money. Liked the girls. Liked the respect it got him in the neighborhood. He especially liked that it seemed to make his father proud.

In that way, Frank too could appreciate what Carlo was saying to him. Bianca had asked him to change, to repent. And he had done it even though it hurt his pride.

It hurt his career. But it saved what was important.

The fact that he'd *forgotten* what was important, even for just a few months, was a stain on his soul. But it could have been worse. He could have done what Carlo did. He could have kept on with the sin, long after he knew it was wrong.

Now, Frank cycled back to the thought that every man made his choices.

And as Frank felt the regret rolling off Carlo in waves, he understood perfectly that some decisions, you couldn't come back from.

CHAPTER 14

It was well after eight when Frank and Carlo emerged from Elias' shop, dressed to the nines in suits that had probably cost more than any of Frank's watches. Even though Elias had made his apologies for giving Frank something off the rack, as far as he was concerned, he looked the best he ever had in his life, weight loss notwithstanding. He'd gone with the navy jacket and trousers with a lighter blue shirt and tie. Carlo had, of course, gone with an almost-black-purple look.

"Kinda look like the Joker, right?" Carlo asked, spinning on his heels, popping his collar.

"Nah, you got flashier than the Joker," he said, forcing a smile even as his heart was still heavy from their conversation in the dressing room.

Carlo smiled, tipping his finger to the brim of his matching fedora.

"I always liked to think so."

They started walking down the street, which was packed with pedestrians bustling past them. Every few feet, it seemed they had to walk under more scaffolding, restricting the already narrow sidewalk. Frank found himself pushed behind Carlo instead of walking beside him.

Typical of New York, no one said 'excuse me' as they squeezed past, not even the ones who shoulder-checked Frank. They didn't even spare him a glance as a silent apology.

Why would they? That was just the way it was here. This was New York. You had to love it or leave it. If you sat around waiting for New York people to change for you, then you'd be having a long wait. But then again… Frank glanced to his side. Was he mistaken in thinking people seemed to give Carlo a bit more space, more leeway to walk without being jostled?

Maybe it had something to do with Carlo looking like a character straight out of the Godfather, or maybe it was because he was so much bigger, but people certainly did seem a lot more careful about moving out of his way. So, Frank stuck close to him, letting him be a human bulldozer as they moved out of the thick of it, and it seemed to work quite well.

Eventually, they came upon a large intersection where they could safely stop without getting run over by angry New Yorkers and hapless disoriented tourists.

Breathing out a relieved sigh, Frank looked down once again at his suit. "Thanks for this, Carlo. I really appreciate it."

"My pleasure. What's the point of any of it if you can't help your friends?" Carlo also seemed to have dimmed since their serious talk, rendering him somehow sadder, more somber, as if he had been the one to confess his worst sin rather than Frank.

Or maybe with the sun setting and it being properly dark now, Carlo was realizing that the day was over, and it would be time to say goodbye soon.

It had to be awkward and uncomfortable. And it had to be upsetting, even for Carlo.

Thanks to their stopover at the scumbag boardwalk pill dealer, Frank now had enough little white tickets to heaven in his pocket to send him off to la-la land whenever he wanted.

No mess. No trouble. No jumping from bridges or putting his gun to his head—if he could somehow get it back from his daughter—and no more thoughts of murderous roller coasters. Now, all he had to do was get back home, maybe run a hot bath to be nice and relaxed, then pop a few of those pills. Lie back, shut his eyes, drift into the next dimension, hopefully not to hell.

"How long has it been since you been to Bensonhurst, Frankie?" Carlo asked, leaning his head to the left, knowing instinctively in which direction their old neighborhood was.

"Honestly, it's been more than thirty years. Longer than the last time I saw you, actually. It may have been at my dad's funeral." Frank furrowed his brow, trying to remember. "Yeah, I think that was it. Notice they've knocked down the old elementary school and put some community garden there. You seen it?"

Carlo threw back his head and laughed. "Yeah, they came to regret that one. The city was pointing to all the people having fewer kids and thought the trend would continue. But then all the Italians started moving out and the Muslims moved in. And those people… Frankie, those people put the Catholics to shame. Breeding machines, I tell you. So now, they're in a bind with too many kids of elementary age and they're scrambling for real estate! Crazy, I tell you."

Frank laughed along with him as they crossed the street, careful to look both ways since the pedestrian signal was flashing red.

"I just never got back over there after my old man's funeral," said Frank, taking a break when they safely crossed, bending down with his hands on his knees to catch his breath. "Other parts of Brooklyn. But not our part."

Carlo moved to the right, using his bulk to once again run defense for Frank as he huffed and gasped to inflate his tired lungs, forcing the other pedestrians to walk around and give him space.

"It's holding up okay. A lot of Chinese though, along with the Muslims."

"Is that a bad thing?" he asked, genuinely not knowing.

Long Island had its fair share of immigrants, but they were all kind of mixed in together. It wasn't segregated in the way the city still was in some parts.

"The Chinese? Nah, not a bad thing at all," said Carlo. "The food's great, and they keep to their own. Well, the Muslims do too. They don't bother us, we don't bother them. But the Jews… they kinda moved out of the neighborhood. Still some left, but not nearly as many. All that bad blood between those two. Not something we get involved with. As long as none of our people get caught in their mess, we don't get involved."

Frank nodded, knowing little about gangland politics, certainly not when it came to the newer immigrant groups. And he didn't want to.

What he really wanted to do was sit down on the curb and just stay there.

It was a cool night. He could tell it was because everyone else was wearing their jackets zipped up. But Frank was sweating, hot and uncomfortable in his expensive suit his old friend had just bought him. He was ready for the night to be over.

He was ready for it *all* to be over. But he could tell Carlo absolutely wasn't.

There was an anxiety about him that hadn't been there before. Maybe even a neediness. Whatever it was, Frank didn't want to be a jerk about it. No need to traumatize Carlo by just flinging himself in front of a Mack truck.

That would be a crappy move. And messy.

"Are uh… you know if my dad's place is still there?" Frank asked, standing up straight and trying to get his balance back.

Slapping him on the back—lightly—Carlo directed him farther down the sidewalk, heading toward Bensonhurst. "Frankie boy, when you see what they done with the place, you'll flip."

He didn't know what that meant, but pretended he did, following Carlo, at least for a block or two. But after that, it was quite clear that Frank wouldn't be able to walk the whole way. It would have been an easy jaunt even two years ago, but now there was just no way.

Carlo set off musing on it all; they should 'just steal some of those hipster e-bikes to teach those punks a lesson about respectable transportation,' he asserted.

Maybe a joke, maybe not; Carlo would have been up for doing it, too, if old decrepit Frankie boy could've hauled his ass onto an e-bike. But there was no chance of that either.

So, Carlo did the reasonable thing and hailed a cab, stepping out into the street and raising his beefy arm into the air. In no time at all, one pulled over, and Frank got to rest easy as they drove into the old neighborhood, turning down all the well-known streets, some looking less familiar than they should, however, before finally arriving at Frank's parents' house.

Or at least it had been, in days gone by.

Gone were the cracked wood siding, the contrasting, faded rain gutters, and the heavy old-fashioned roof shingles.

"Well, I guess the old neighborhood came up in the world," he marveled, looking at the masterful restoration of his childhood home. She looked beautiful.

"Yeah, these young kids gentrified it good and proper," Carlo agreed, appraising the bay windows, crisp vinyl siding and meticulously maintained lawns with approval. "Fully detached houses are going for over a million dollars these days. Now, my old house, it got wrecked to put in a block of townhouses. But those are expensive as hell too. Over a million for a 1920s house that a factory worker supported on one salary."

Frank shook his head, gobsmacked at what a difference a single generation made.

"How do young families do it?" he asked, not even expecting a response. It was meant as a rhetorical question.

"They don't, Frankie," said Carlo, his tone going sad again. "You said your middle girl is married now? I bet she don't have a house."

"Nope. An apartment. They're worried if it'll be good for a baby."

"Hell no, it won't be good for a baby. Kids need space and fresh air. I tell you, if I had to do it over again, I'd have taken every one of my kids and all their screeching-bitch mothers and relocated us all to Utah or something. This city's no good for any of us."

Frank didn't look directly at Carlo, just slid his eyes over to see if he appeared as serious as he sounded. He did. Even with Carlo's hands in his pockets, Frank could see they were clenched into fists as he stared up at Frank's old house, something like longing, frustration, and deep regret creasing his face.

"We're both Brooklyn boys, Carlo," Frank said, trying to sound soothing. "The farthest I ever got was Long Island."

"Yeah, but it was far enough. Far enough to make something of yourself and do right by your family. That's nothing to sneeze at."

"Still..." He tried to think of something to pull Carlo out of whatever funk he had sunk into. "Those prices are crazy. It's part of why I moved out of the city."

It wasn't just that though.

As Frank looked up at his parents' old house, even with the modern facelift, part of him felt disquieted just standing on this street again. Uneasy, anxious, as though he shouldn't be there.

Seeming to notice, Carlo gave him a light shove, getting them moving once again.

"I feel the same way. Before they knocked it down, I drove past my old house every once in a while. But I never walked by on foot. Never stopped in front or nothing like that. It just feels funny, going back to where you lived as a kid. Even though I just live across town. It's like wearing clothes that are too small. I guess we're supposed to leave all that behind."

"Clothes that are too small?" Frank asked, taking Carlo back to what he'd just said. "More like clothes you thought were yours but ain't," Frank agreed, liking the analogy.

The phases of Frank's life could be marked by distinct locations: which school he'd attended, which place he'd been working at and, of course, where he'd been living. The funny thing was that even for the places holding overall good memories, such as his parents' house, he'd never felt a need to return, never pined for 'the good old days' or wished he'd chosen a different path.

As he walked down the sidewalk, this time beside Carlo instead of behind him, it was clear that wasn't the case with him. Despite his style and bravado, it seemed to Frank that Carlo had a lot of regrets. He didn't like to come back to the old neighborhood not because he'd outgrown it, but because he wanted to go back to when he'd lived there—and make a few changes.

Frank knew that burden, but only in terms of betraying Bianca. He'd take that back if he could, even if he had to give something up to do it. But Carlo… maybe it was his whole life he regretted. Which was a terrible feeling, one that Frank didn't envy.

The thing about gentrified neighborhoods was that they loved to stuff as many types of businesses into a city block as possible.

After he and Carlo crossed the street, they moved into a commercial block, leaving the residences behind, to find themselves passing a Chinese restaurant, a tailor's shop, a computer and cell phone repair shop, and finally, at the end of the next block, an art gallery of all things.

Never one for art—Bianca took care of the decorating—Frank had never been inside a gallery, not even after meeting all those movers and shakers at the Manhattan insurance firm. But for some reason, he came to a stop outside the gallery anyway.

He peered inside for some reason, never expecting to see anything he liked in such a place.

Seeing him pause, Carlo backpedaled, stepping back onto the curb.

"You wanna go inside?" he asked dubiously, squinting in through the windows as though expecting a hitman to emerge from the shadows.

"Yeah," said Frank, reaching for the door. "I think I do."

He wasn't sure why, but something about the colorful painting in the window—some abstract configuration of a cupcake of all things—drew him in.

As soon he opened the door, a blast of cool air hit him, making him sigh in contentment.

"Damn place is an icebox," snapped Carlo, crossing his arms immediately.

Not another soul was in the small gallery, which was odd. "Aren't they worried somebody could steal something?" Frank wondered aloud.

Nodding up at the cameras, Carlo responded, "I don't imagine these have much street value. The cameras are enough of a deterrent against random kids being assholes."

Carlo was visibly uncomfortable.

He didn't follow Frank over to the first painting hanging on the wall. Instead, he remained in front of the door, hands in his pockets, and shifting his weight from foot to foot, obviously just waiting for Frank to look around and be done with it.

Fair enough.

As Frank eyed the first work, a massive rectangular canvas with no frame, showing a bright, swirling image of a bar back, he decided it was definitely the colors that had spoken to him.

The way the bottles of liquor in the painting were simultaneously blurry and yet so bright and vibrant; it was all so beautiful and not like anything else he had seen in his life.

Definitely not like the prints of classic works Bianca had hanging in the house.

The paintings all looked to be done by the same artist.

He moved onto the next one, this one a rainy street in what looked like an Asian city. It was beautiful too, and not like that new stuff that they put in the Museum of Modern Art, which was random paint splashes or regular garbage. A torn-up armchair or wrecked pair of musty old shoes. More than once, Frank had read a news story about some modern art masterpiece getting tossed because an over-eager janitor had rightly assumed it was trash.

But this place wasn't like that. His eyes drifted down to the placard beneath the rainy street painting: Annabella Duarte.

He smiled. *Another Annabella. No surprise there. I'll have to tell 'my' Annabella about this.*

Except... no, Frank corrected himself. He wouldn't be telling her about it. Or anything else. He had told her all he ever would. And he just hoped it was enough.

Swallowing hard, Frank continued his slow progression down the line, from one painting to the next. All had different subjects but were expressed in the same way—swirls of color and a blurry effect strategically deployed to control what the viewer focused on.

It was like van Gogh, but with an update. He liked it a lot.

The gallery led him in a u-shaped rectangle to the back wall of the gallery, and then up the opposite wall, back toward the front entrance.

Carlo started inching backward toward the door, visibly relieved Frank was almost done walking the loop. At the last painting, he came to a halt, taking a double take at the blurry, yet colorful portrait of a woman, her hair bundled up in a Gibson-girl bun as she stared longingly out of a snow-covered window, a cigarette clenched tightly in her hand.

"This one looks like my mom," he said hoarsely, stepping closer to the painting, trying to make sure it really was his mother.

But the closer he got, the harder it was to make out the lines of her face.

"She does kinda favor her a little," Carlo admitted, coming a little closer. "But not that much. Hair's all wrong to be sure. Though your mom did love her Virginia Slims. That, I remember."

Despite the air conditioner being on full blast, Frank once again felt a wave of heat blasting out of his collar and he stepped away from the painting, blinking several times to try and clear the vision of his mother.

"Pop?" a voice whispered in his ear.

"Annabella?" He spun around, slack-jawed, terrified his daughter had found him.

"Whoa there!" Carlo grabbed Frank's shoulders, steadying him before he fell, face creased in concern as he peered at him. "You need another pill, Frankie? You don't look so good."

"Nah, I think I better not," he said, feeling short of breath and claustrophobic.

But at the same time, it was cooler in the gallery than outside, so if he stepped out, he might feel worse.

Grabbing onto Carlo's shoulder for support, he turned around, where a dividing wall stood between the two sides of the gallery. He jolted back.

"Jesus!" he gasped, eyes going wide at the massive painting hanging in vivid color on the dividing wall.

It was him. Frank Vitale, standing in a bar… right next to Carlo Sanguinetti.

Feeling as if a vice was tightening around his heart, he backed away from the painting, his mouth stretched wide in horror.

It was them. The way they'd looked on that last horrible day, arguing over the phone as Frank told Carlo he couldn't help him with his 'business' anymore and to never call him again.

The painting perfectly captured Carlo's face, the storm of embittered anger clear as day painted onto his younger, thinner features as he stood leaning against the bar.

"Handsome devils, aren't we? A lot better than the mirror on the boardwalk, that's for sure." Carlo slung an arm around Frank's shoulder and beamed at him. "No need to be scared of your own reflection, Frankie."

"What?" He looked at Carlo, then back at the painting of them, blinking rapidly as sweat ran into his eyes.

It wasn't a painting. It was a floor-length mirror, the only color coming from his own reflection and the looping vinyl script affixed to the top left corner of the glass

Welcome to Bensonhurst Gallery.

Breathing hard, he forced a laugh, embarrassed and concerned for his own state of mind. "Yeah, I guess we are handsome. A far sight better than those Bermuda shorts we were in."

You're losing it, Frank.

First his mother, then a scene from his own past.

Somehow, he was losing his grip on his senses. But he could have sworn what he saw was real. His reflection in the mirror showed two old men, one fat, ruddy, and obviously in failing health, the other one dangerously thin, and obviously dying.

The painting had been two middle-aged guys: thinner, younger, dressed differently.

He was so sure…

"Well, I don't know about you, but that's enough high culture for me today," Frank laughed, still not sure what to say, or what was happening to him.

Carlo nodded, looking uncomfortable, as if unsure what to do with his hands.

"Sounds great to me. As a matter of fact, I got someplace we'll feel more at home, a little lower culture if you know what I mean."

Frank nodded and followed Carlo out of the gallery, casting one last glance over his shoulder to make sure the mirror was in fact a mirror, and hadn't reverted back to that cursed painting.

It was. Just. A. Mirror. That was all.

Just a mirror, Frank. Just a mirror.

Together, they walked down the sidewalk, the crowd thinner than when they'd entered.

CHAPTER 15

When Carlo said he knew a place with *lower* culture, Frank's first thought had been that he was about to be dragged into a strip club. Even as a young, single man, he had never liked those places. Far from the sexy and exciting joints most of his friends thought they were, every time Frank saw one of those places, or the poor girls who worked there, only sadness came forth.

Now that he was a father of girls, he hated them even more.

The only occasion on which Daniella had ever listened to him the first time around was right before she'd gone off to college. As she was eighteen, some girl she'd met at school had tried to tell her that being a stripper was a good 'summer job.'

Not one of her regular friends. Some gross girl who had never been over to the house before, trying to lead his daughter astray. Well, he was having none of it. Who did she think she was? Of course, he never expected Daniella to listen to him. Not ever.

Frank had put his foot down right then and there anyway, telling her all about what kind of life strippers lived. Even the ones at the supposedly upscale places. Drugs, bikers, pimps… it was bad all around. And more times than not, those girls then got fed into the porn pipeline.

And who knew where that could end? No, no, no, she mustn't do it!

Daniella had listened to him without interrupting for a change.

Her head tilted side to side like a dog listening to its master. She narrowed her eyes, evaluating. Then, his eyes almost dropped from his head to hear her say, nodding, "Thanks Dad. You're right, I won't do it. And I'll tell her it was a stupid idea as well." Then, she'd leaned toward him and whispered, "Don't tell Mom I even asked, okay?"

And he hadn't. Maybe he should have, but Bianca would have hit the roof. It was probably the only occasion on which Daniella had specifically sought his advice. And he was glad to give it, relieved beyond all reason she hadn't gone ahead with it. To have his girl in such a job, he'd never have slept at night again. But she had listened to him, her father.

So, he wasn't about to ruin that moment by telling Bianca when she'd asked him not to.

With all that in mind, he wasn't about to participate in objectifying someone else's daughter at one of those places.

Luckily, that wasn't what Carlo had in mind.

"There she is," he said proudly, sweeping his arm in grandiose fashion, as though pulling a curtain back. There, across the street, was a regular bar—no sign of naked ladies, drug dealers, or hanky panky of any kind. Actually, it looked more like the kind of neighborhood bar the old timers would go to for smokes, a stiff drink, and to catch up on what the young people were doing these days. Frank loved it immediately.

Long Island had its charms, but a proper neighborhood bar wasn't one of them.

They were all those newfangled mixology sorts of places, with the bartenders being young ladies wearing tank tops, tattoos all up and down their arms, shaking up drinks with weird names and about seven hundred ingredients in them.

This place looked like something out of the late 1980s, a squat brick place wedged into the corner of a larger building like a piece of pie, and even though there were no windows in the front, Frank imagined the bartender was probably a balding guy named Mort.

The blue neon sign above the door reading *Paradiso* was the only indication it was a business at all. Exactly the way it should be as far as Frank was concerned.

"This your regular haunt?" Frank asked, making it clear with his tone that he approved.

"Only recently," Carlo replied. "I had another place closer to my house, but this one…. This is my bar now."

Nodding, Frank stepped out into the road, his eye on the pretty blue sign.

He could definitely use a drink.

The pavement in front lit up as he walked, and the sound of a blaring horn jerked his head up.

Blinded by headlights barreling toward him, his surroundings bleached out, going completely white as the horn consumed his hearing.

"Frank!"

In a flash, he was back in his car, Bianca beside him, her purse in her lap, and her arm outstretched as she screamed in horror at the truck barreling down on them.

In slow motion, Frank reached for her, taking his hands off the wheel, his foot off the brake. He could think of nothing but shielding her with his body.

But his fingers grabbed nothing but air; he didn't get so much as a touch of her before the deafening crash jolted him at an angle that should have snapped his back, flinging him like a rag doll until a crushing weight on his chest brought him to a halt.

Time seemed to stop as everything went black, only for it to start up again in flashes, jerking Frank from one moment to the next, completely ignorant of what passed between each moment of consciousness. The sound of his heart beating, his breaths coming in great gasps, he couldn't hear Bianca anymore at all. No screaming. No gasping. No breathing from her at all.

Red and blue lights. Pain. And the sound of a saw cutting through metal.

"My wife…" he croaked out, blurry figures fading in and out of his sight.

"We'll get her out, buddy, don't worry," said a male voice, sounding far away.

Then more voices, a sensation of motion, and lights above as he was wheeled on a gurney down a hallway. "Male patient, sixty plus, compound fractures, blood loss. They didn't bring the wallet in with him, so we don't have anything yet." This one was a female voice, older. The sound of her voice echoed as Frank struggled to open his eyes.

But it was so bright. And everything hurt so much.

"We got six more who came in too. The wreck was a real pile-up."

Where's Bianca? Work on her, don't work on me!

"All right, prep for surgery."

The motion stopped, and there was the sound of a curtain being pulled back.

Willing his eyes open, Frank could see the hospital all around him, even as he struggled to understand what was happening.

I need help, he thought, but couldn't speak.

He needed to know where Bianca was. Did they take her to the same hospital?

Turning his head to the side, there was another man lying on a bed, blood staining his face, eyes open as he stared at the ceiling.

Carlo?

"Damn it, Frank!"

The horn blared as the truck sped past him, missing him by inches as he was violently jerked back onto the sidewalk.

Breathing hard, Frank whipped his head around to see Carlo holding the back of his shirt, his face turned stark white in panic.

"What the hell you doing just stepping out in the road? You trying to check out early on me? Jesus, you really wanna go like that?" Carlo shouted, his eyes bulging in disbelief.

"I didn't... I didn't see the truck," Frank sputtered out, tears springing to his eyes. "I didn't see it. I would have moved if I'd seen it."

Bianca had been so close. Right next to him!

Carlo let go of his collar as he dropped to the ground, sitting on the curb with his face in his hands. He swore he could still smell her perfume. He didn't try to fight back the tears. And he couldn't bring himself to tell Carlo what he'd seen as he stared down the headlights, as he'd once again inadvertently stepped in front of a truck.

He was so tired, so tired he couldn't bear it.

All he wanted was to see Bianca again. For real. Not in some crazy hallucination of the day that basically ended his life. It was like something out of hell sent to punish him, making him relive his helplessness as he watched her die.

"Ah, Frankie, it's all right," Carlo said and sighed, dropping down on the curb next to him, laying a hand on his shoulder.

"I just... I didn't see it," Frank said again, wiping his face, trying to get a hold of himself. "I think those pills are stronger than the ones the doctor gave me. A higher dose maybe. When I looked into the headlights, I remembered being in the hospital after the wreck." He sniffed, wiping the last of the tears from his eyes. "And then you were there too for some reason. I might be high right now. Probably why I didn't see the truck."

"That right?" Carlo asked, his tone tight. He was still breathing hard too.

"Sorry I gave you a scare," he said, looking over at Carlo apologetically.

His face was still white, sweat beading up on his forehead and his mouth pressed thin.

The man looked so shaken, Frank felt bad. He would have been relieved to have the truck take him out, but he didn't want to scar Carlo in the process. Or anyone else.

Certainly, he didn't want to make trouble for a truck driver trying to earn an honest living.

Carlo took a deep breath, seeming as if he was trying to gather himself too, trying to force some level of normalcy back into his tone.

"No worries, Frankie. I guess the good thing about being on the way out is you can drink with your pills and it's no big deal. So, let's get one, shall we?"

Frank nodded, honestly looking forward to a stiff drink. Carlo looked as if he needed one too.

Holding onto Carlo for support, he got to his feet and, this time, they both looked left, right, then left again before they crossed the street to get to the blue neon-lit entrance to Paradiso.

Carlo held the door open for him and tilted his head to the side.

"Come on in. Let's get a drink. One last time."

CHAPTER 16

A plume of smoke hit Frank right in the face as he and Carlo walked through the door of the Paradiso. Apparently, New York City's smoking ban didn't apply here. Or maybe, Frank thought as he took a good look at the patronage, they didn't care what the laws were.

From the outside, Frank had admired the fact that the bar looked like something from the past, a relic from an era long gone by and mostly forgotten. The inside was exactly the same. Exposed brick walls, knock-off Tiffany lamps hanging over the booths, casting a red and green pall over the faces of the men who sat there. And they *were* almost all men.

The four top tables in the middle of the room all wobbled with every movement of the people who sat there, the wood varnish peeling and stained.

The vinyl in the booths had tears in them, and the floor, from the looks of it, had once had a pattern in the tile, but now it was mostly worn away. It was sticky underfoot, as expected.

The only woman was a middle-aged lady behind the bar, her enormous cleavage partially exposed, but not to be alluring. It was simply because no shirt could reasonably contain all of that; it was like an airbag that had burst.

If he had to guess, Frank pegged her for Italian, or maybe Greek.

Thick-boned, dark and curly hair piled on top of her head, and her hands were adorned with multiple rings per finger, topped off by long red nails. Real ones. Not those disgusting clacky press-ons the young girls wore.

Even though she didn't have a cigarette hanging from her lip, she looked as though she ought to. "Carlo," she called out, looking up from her drink-making activities. "How are you, honey? I see you brought a friend."

"We can always use more friends here!' one of the barflies yelled, bringing forth a chorus of derisive laughter from some of the other patrons.

The guys in the bar all looked to be some level of scummy. The ones at the bar were more along the lines of drug dealers, while the older and more imposing men at the booths looked distinctively like wise guys.

Is this a mob bar? He began inching closer to the big-chested bartender, feeling as if he needed a drink more than ever.

"How 'bout you pour us some rum and Cokes there, gorgeous?" Carlo said, making eyes at the lady bartender as he heaved himself onto one of the stools.

Still looking around in wonder, Frank sat down beside him, trying not to let his eyes linger on any one person for too long. He definitely didn't want to come off as looking for trouble.

Not in a place like this. But then again, it would almost certainly guarantee his demise.

"So, what do you think of this place, Frankie? Or our girl, Maddie?" Carlo leaned his head at the bartender, who was already pouring their rum and cokes.

"Well… I didn't think places like this existed. Thought all the real bars went away with the smoking ban," he managed, loosening his tie. It was hot as blazes in the bar and Frank wasn't sure how much longer he could tolerate it.

"There's still some special places around the city," Maddie said, setting the drinks down in front of them. "Just have to know where to look. What's your name, sweetie?" she asked him.

Carlo slapped him on the shoulder. "This is Frank Vitale. He was a kid from the neighborhood, but he grew up and made good. Not like the rest of us."

"Then what the hell is he doing here?" Maddie asked, a sly smile working its way across her face.

"He's just slumming it with me for the night," Carlo cracked back, not missing a beat.

"Well, welcome to Paradiso," she said, giving a nod before heading across the bar.

"Where's the paradise part?" he whispered into Carlo's ear, leaning closer so no one else could hear his question.

"Seek and ye shall find, I guess. Drink up, Frankie."

Smiling at his friend, Frank clinked glasses with Carlo, knocking back his cocktail in two swigs.

"How about a couple shots, Maddie?" Carlo bellowed, raising his empty glass in the air.

Frank winced at the rudeness of it, but Maddie hollered right back from across the room, "Little early in the night, Carlo. You hang in long enough, I'll allow it. You stick with the cocktails for now. Hang tight. I'll get you and your friend another one."

She went back to taking the drink order of the sad-looking man at the other side of the bar. He looked so sad, in fact, Frank had to suppress the urge to pick up the man's tab.

Tipping his hat in gratitude, Carlo set the empty glass back on the bar. "She's a good girl, that Maddie. Too good to be here," he said a little more quietly, pushing the brim of his hat back so he could get his face closer to Frank's ear. "But I suppose she's got a past and that's why she's here, pouring drinks to us bums. Shame, really."

"Everyone's got a past," said Frank, not sure what was so bad about being a bartender. Or maybe Carlo meant it was bad to be a bartender at this specific place?

Carlo was about to say something else when heavy footsteps sounded on the floor behind them. Frank turned to see one of the wise guys from the corner booth standing over him, leering down at Frank as though he owed him money.

He was a stranger; Frank had never seen him before. But obviously Carlo had.

"No one invited you over here, Joey. Why don't you crawl back where you came from," he sneered, staying seated on the stool, but turning around to face the man, his shoulders squared in such a way as to communicate there would be violence if he wasn't obeyed.

The man didn't so much as look at Carlo.

"So, you're Frank," he said, stretching his face in a nasty smile as he looked down at him. "*The* Frank. Not what I expected, I gotta say. You don't look so special to me."

A chill crept down Frank's spine as he stared back, determined not to be cowed by this man he didn't know… But who very clearly knew him.

"Pretty sure I don't know you, buddy," said Frank, reaching far back in his memory and reviving the body language of a Brooklyn kid who didn't take shit from anyone. He stood up and looked down at the man, letting his eyes slowly drift up and down his smaller, slimmer body.

You're older than me, he let his eyes say. *And you look even closer to death than I do. You sure you want a problem?*

All this he said with nothing more than the set of his jaw and the narrowing of his eyes.

But this Joey character was obviously from a similar neighborhood. He understood perfectly.

"Settle down, fella. My days of bar tussles are far behind me. Probably for you too." He slid his eyes over to Carlo. "I just heard so much about you, I wanted to meet you. Pity Carlo never told you about me."

"Give it a rest, Joey," Carlo cut in, the gaunt, pale look on his face returning in force. Far from the brash wise guy who had threatened to beat up the red-headed Mexican who bumped into him on the boardwalk, Carlo now looked like a schoolboy about to be scolded.

This Joey guy was obviously drunk. And obviously looking for a problem. But he was old enough to be Frank's dad. Maybe in his eighties. And from the way Carlo was acting, he could only assume he was higher up in the mob food chain. Maybe at the very top.

Lucky for Frank, things like that didn't bother him anymore.

"Who is this clown?" Frank asked, turning his head toward Carlo, but not his body, so he could still see the prick out of the corner of his eye in case he tried anything. He was thoroughly annoyed at this crap now, almost hoping the old coot took a swing at him.

He was just trying to have a nice drink with his friend—the last one he'd ever have—and some elder statesman of thuggery was over here causing a problem. How did any guy get into his eighties and still act like this?

"Giuseppe Bartolucci," said Joey, sticking his hand out. "I'm the one who made Carlo. And the one who unmade him." He dropped his hand, seeming to get the hint that Frank wouldn't be shaking it. "Or actually, *you* were the one who unmade him, Frank. You and your little stunt."

Carlo's eyes got even wider, and his mouth pressed into a tight, thin line.

What the hell is he talking about?

Turning his head back toward Joey, he gave the old geezer a fixed stare that made it clear he had better get to the point quickly. "Like I said, pal. I don't know you. So, any stunts I've pulled in my time got nothing to do with you."

"One of them did. All those insurance policies you were fixing for Carlo? You were actually fixing those for me." He leaned back, resting his hand on his own chest, giving a faux bashful smile. "Carlo here was just the in-between guy. See, it never mattered how much money I made; there was no insurance broker having me over to his house for dinner, that's for sure.

"But then you decided to grow a conscience and instead of dealing with your attitude, like I told him to…" Joey slid a disgusted sneer in Carlo's direction. "This guy, he just decided to shrug it off. Like it was nothing. Like you hadn't just ripped millions of dollars out of my pocket. So, it seemed only fair I make him nothing in return."

Oh no. Finally, Frank understood who this lowlife was. He was Carlo's boss. The guy he had to answer to. Which meant he was probably a friend of Carlo's father.

Which explained why Carlo wasn't saying anything. He seemed to have folded into himself, looking down into his lap, clearly just waiting for Joey to go away.

Frank sighed. Just today, he had asked Carlo if he'd caused a problem for him by backing out of their arrangement all those years ago. And Carlo had said no. But that didn't seem to be the case. At the time, he hadn't even given it a thought. All he had on his mind was what Bianca might say to someone about what he was doing. He'd still been working at Turner then. His job was his world, his identity. So, with Bianca demanding he stop doing it, he had to listen.

The stakes were too high.

The next time Carlo had called his office phone for a favor, Frank had told him no. He remembered it like it was yesterday. "This isn't going to work out, Carlo. It's bringing too much heat on me, and that's without even getting caught. It's only a matter of time and I don't want it. We're done. For good. And I think it's best you don't ever call me again."

Who the hell do you think you are? Carlo had raged. *You think that job makes you something special? You're the same trash you were when I picked your ass up off the pavement!*

But he had stood his ground. It didn't matter how much access he had to the internal systems. He wouldn't be adding a beneficiary's name to any more policies after a policyholder had died.

His whole frame of mind in the lead-up to their discussion was what Carlo would think of him. How mad he would be. And if he would do something to Frank in retaliation. For some reason, it never occurred to him that Carlo would have to answer to someone. That he might be endangering someone else with his decision.

"It wasn't a problem," Carlo had said earlier today.

But it had been. A big problem.

But that didn't mean Joey got to come over here and dig up old issues. Not tonight.

"Well, just outta curiosity," Frank asked, fixing his face so the little prick didn't know he'd gotten to him. "How exactly did you want Carlo to fix my attitude?"

Though he was facing away from the bar, Frank could feel Maddie freeze behind him, and the rest of the patrons sitting at the bar who were close enough to hear subtly leaned away, placing one foot down on the floor. He knew that stance well. It was the move of someone getting ready to run away fast if something popped off.

"Just a man-to-man conversation between two friends, of course," Joey lied, smiling like a used car salesman. "But I understand, he didn't want to push. And hey, I didn't want to push either. So, I just moved him to a job more in line with his skill set. Something that didn't require even a hint of balls. You wanna know what it was?"

"You're cut off, Joey," said Maddie quietly. "You go sit down. I'll bring you a Coke?"

"I'll let you know when I've had enough!" roared Joey, diverting his gaze only briefly to Maddie over Frank's shoulder before returning to the topic at hand. "Did Carlo ever tell you what I had him do after you welched on fixing those insurance policies?"

"I don't know, rousting drunks outta the strip clubs?" Frank shot back, subtly moving himself between Joey and Carlo.

"We had another scam going on down at the horse track," Joey explained, the smile morphing into one of happy nostalgia, as if telling his grandkid about the good old days. "See back then, it was easier to fix the races. All you had to do was dope up the horses so they threw the race. The trainers knew to look for needle marks or if you put something in the food. So, we knew not to do that. So, what you had to do was stick the drugs up the horses' keister."

He threw his head back and roared with laughter. "That became Carlo's job, and he was damn good at it. Damn good!" Joey laughed.

Frank curled his fist, ready to throw whatever energy was left into knocking Joey's teeth out.

He kept his eyes plastered on Joey's face because, honestly, he didn't have the stomach to turn and look at Carlo. Shame and embarrassment were radiating off him, and he could imagine the look on his face well enough. He didn't need to actually see it.

He had shamed his friend, made him lose face with his organization. And unlike Frank, who would have just suffered a few minor indignities if he'd gotten caught fixing those policies, Carlo had had to answer to the mob. He'd even gone so far as to refuse to hurt Frank because of it. He'd gone against what his boss had told him to do.

Old Joey didn't look so tough now, but twenty years ago, he'd probably been a force to be reckoned with. And it was clear Carlo had paid dearly for Frank backing out.

"Why don't you get the hell out of here, Joey?" Carlo said, sounding as though he'd just been punched in the throat.

"Why? I got nowhere else to be. And neither do you," slurred Joey, spreading his arms out, gesturing at the sad bar and its many washed-up mobsters. "None of us got no other place to be."

The smile finally dropped from the asshole's face, replaced by an expression of remorse, maybe even a touch of jealousy as he looked Frank up and down once more. "But maybe you do, huh? Maybe you get to be somewhere else. Good for you."

Without another word, Joey turned and walked back toward the entrance, teetering slightly as he gracelessly slid back into the farthest booth.

The whole bar seemed to exhale in relief when he sat down.

Blowing out a long breath, Frank finally turned back toward Carlo. He looked exactly as he'd imagined. Sad, looking down into his hands folded in his lap. He couldn't have looked more ashamed if he had actually been caught stealing from the church.

His adrenaline had kicked in with his anger at Joey, briefly clearing his head from the pills, and then from the drink he'd had on top of it.

But now he was feeling woozy again too as the sensation wore off.

"I'm so sorry, Carlo. I was a selfish prick. I shouldn't —"

"You have nothing to be sorry about." He cut him off but still didn't look up. "I'm the sorry rat bastard. Not you. It's like I told you back at Elias' place, Frank. You're a good man. Always were." He looked up, but not at Frank. Instead, he let his eyes drift over the bar. "And that's why I belong here. And you don't."

Frank looked around the bar full of miserable old men and one woman, all of them looking as though they'd rather be someplace else. Anywhere else.

"But you don't have to stay, Carlo. It ain't too late for you either."

Carlo just smiled sadly and then let out a loud, relieved sigh as Maddie poured out another batch of cocktails for them. And this time, a shot.

"Drink up, Frank."

CHAPTER 17

It didn't take very long for Frank's head, already fuzzy from the pills, to start swimming like a salmon in a whirlpool. Carlo remained fairly quiet, strangely introspective. His only words were directed at Maddie as he called out for yet another drink. After three rounds of shots, she cut him off, but compromised by pouring the weakest Scotch and soda Frank had ever seen.

Frank himself had drunk only the one shot and that was enough to know even that one had been a mistake. Maddie, being the lifelong bartender she was, didn't even need Frank to give her instructions; she just followed up with a ginger ale. How she knew his soda of choice was a mystery. It was possible she was just that good.

The mood in the bar was similarly somber, though even in his compromised state, Frank could guess that was normal. It had nothing to do with Joey's little performance with Carlo.

This wasn't a place people came to so they could have a good time, was it?

They came here to forget. But once they got here, they were rarely successful. Instead, they downed their drinks in a cloud of rumination and regret.

He now understood why Carlo had started coming here.

Even though standing was going to be a dangerous proposition, Frank needed to go to the men's room. He'd held it as long as he'd dared, and waiting was no longer an option.

"I'm gonna hit the can, Carlo," he said, leaning in and holding onto his friend's shoulder as he rose from the stool.

"Want me to come with you?" Carlo was slurring his words now.

"Nah, I'll just lean against the wall. Just like the good old days," he said, trying to crack a smile. The bathroom wasn't far away, but Frank took his time, grabbing onto the bar as much as he could, then the backs of empty chairs, finally reaching out for the wall for the last few feet.

He felt sorry for all the germophobes who never wanted to touch anything in public restrooms; in Frank's view, there were few things as satisfying as leaning forward and resting your head against the cool tile behind the urinal while you took a piss you'd been holding in.

Luckily, there was no one else in the men's room, or else they might have been weirded out when Frank let out a loud, "ahhh."

When he was done, he was careful to take his time once again, none of his dizziness or the seeming time lag in his vision having cleared. If anything, it was worse. Maybe it was because he'd just taken a piss. After all, what remained in his system had to be less diluted now, didn't it?

Going over to the sink, he washed his hands. Then, for good measure, he bent over and splashed water on his face, rubbing his eyes in the hope of clearing his head just a little.

I wonder if Maddie's got coffee back there.

Probably not. As far as he knew, no bar he had ever been to served coffee. You'd think it would be good for business. Get buzzed, sober up with a nice cup of joe, then drink more to get buzzed all over again. Maybe it wasn't that simple. Maybe mixing coffee and cocktails was a recipe for vomiting or something.

The door to the john squeaked as he straightened up. He turned to seek out the paper towel dispenser, and there was Carlo, standing in the doorway as if propping it up.

The sight of him sent a jolt of terror through Frank's body.

Dark brown blood was crusted all over Carlo's face, stains and scabs covering his cheeks and nose, and even his ears, the mess all cascading from a single, massive gash right through the middle of Carlo's forehead as if he'd been struck by a cleaver.

Or maybe like he'd smashed his head into a steering wheel.

Frank stumbled back, gasping at the sight before dropping his face into his hands, giving his eyes a good rub, trying to catch his breath.

"It's all right, Frankie. I got you."

Feeling Carlo's hands on his shoulders, he looked up once more, blinking rapidly to clear his vision.

The dried blood and the gash were gone.

Carlo's face looked normal again, no sign of dried blood or the horrible injury. It no longer resembled the hallucination he'd had of him in the hospital bed.

"Sorry…" he breathed out, not feeling well at all. Not just woozy anymore, but as if his whole body had pins and needles in it. Not exactly like the seizures, but a weird feeling. "Listen, Carlo, can we get out of here? Get some fresh air?"

"That's probably a good idea. They got some tables outside. Probably a little chilly for that tonight but…" He nodded at Frank's forehead, covered in sweat. "Probably no issue for you."

"You got that right."

Any semblance of pride in Frank had gone right out the window as Carlo kept his arm around his shoulders, escorting him carefully out of the men's room.

But now, instead of turning right to go back to the bar, Carlo directed them left, down a narrow, dimly lit hallway with no pictures or decorations on its raw brick walls. At the end of the hallway was a heavy black door, a painted sign with the bar name hanging over the frame.

Paradiso.

The breeze blasted him in the face as Carlo pushed the door open, bringing them out onto a small patio, four concrete tables gathered in a circle, and a wrought-iron gate surrounding it. The view was hardly spectacular—a patio overlooking the alley. With all the dumpsters.

"I guess that answers why no one sits out here," he said as Carlo eased him down at one of the tables.

"Yeah, it's not exactly Central Park." He nodded at the gate. "But it gets you where you wanna go."

Carlo sat beside him and together, they stared into the ugly alley. Without the distraction of the constantly incoming drinks, Carlo seemed at a loss for what to do or say.

"What Joey said…" Frank started, tentative in his tone. "I really am sorry. I know you understand why I backed out in hindsight. But you must have been real mad at me at the time."

Carlo sat stock still, his breathing loud and labored.

He's probably deciding how bad he'd feel if he just decked me in the face.

Finally, Carlo nodded, keeping his gaze fixed straight ahead. "Yeah, of course; I was mad. It's easier to get pissed at someone else instead of yourself. Why look at my life decisions when I can just point at yours? Classic deflection." He let out a grunt of a laugh. "Katerina, my third ex, she liked to read all those self-help books. She'd call me out every time we had an argument. 'You're deflecting, Carlo!' Used to get pissed at her a lot too. But she was right. My fatal flaw."

Frank nodded, but something about Carlo had been bugging him all day. From the very start, something had been nagging at him that just didn't seem right. Even now in his drug and booze haze, the unsettled feeling was there, louder than ever, at the back of his brain.

"Why were you at Coney Island today? Were you there looking for me?"

He kept his tone curious, rather than accusatory.

He wasn't afraid of his old friend. He had no reason to be afraid of much of anything at this point. But he needed to know. It was just too big of a coincidence running into him today.

Carlo's half smile somewhat confirmed his suspicions.

"I feel like I've been looking for you for a long time,' he said cryptically, staring off into middle space. "Just wandering places. The old neighborhood. Downtown

Manhattan, around your old office. Then today, the boardwalk just seemed the place to go. And there you were."

Carlo sat silently for a moment, still not looking at him. After a while, he looked down, and fished a half chewed-down cigar and a Zippo out of his jacket pocket.

He took his time lighting the cigar, then took a long drag on it, blowing the smoke up into the air and trying not to let it drift into Frank's face.

"The funny thing was how long it took to find you. The last time I saw you, I wasn't looking for you at all. You just dropped right into my line of sight. Like destiny."

Frank squinted at him, turning his head quicker than he should have, bringing on a fresh wave of dizziness. Taking a deep breath to set his equilibrium right again, he asked, "What do you mean? The last time we talked before today was over the phone, wasn't it? The last time we saw each other was what… the week before over drinks?"

Carlo shook his head. "That was the last time *you* saw *me*. Not the last time I saw you."

Well, this is weird, thought Frank. *The old boy's definitely had his fill of drink. Nothing he says makes any sense anymore.*

Still staring straight ahead, Carlo took another drag on his cigar, Frank patiently waiting, understanding perfectly he wasn't going to like what he was about to hear. Or maybe he would. Maybe it'd be the story about that one time Carlo planned to kill him, then changed his mind.

Or maybe that had been the plan for today. Maybe that was why he was so accommodating when Frank told him his plan for a final day.

"It was about a year ago," Carlo said. "I don't get out to Long Island much. Nothing there for me, just a bunch of suburbs. But Katerina, you know, the ex who said I always deflected? She lives out there. She broke her ankle, and I went out to see her. Stopped at the store to get her some snacks. She was too embarrassed to use that motorized cart." He blew out a large plume of smoke and finally turned to look at Frank, a bone-deep sadness weighing down his features.

"And it was the damnedest thing. I saw you and Bianca there."

Frank felt his stomach drop.

A year ago.

The grocery store.

What was Carlo going to say to him? Even as Frank's eyes widened to damn near take up his whole face, he kept quiet, waiting for him to continue.

"It all came flooding back, you know?" Carlo said, spreading his hands out in front of him, as if he had sand slipping through his fingers. "That call we had. And everything that happened afterward. I thought I'd moved on. But then there you were. You and Bianca. You looked like you didn't have a care in the world…"

"And you thought you'd give me one?" Frank asked, his tone darkening.

"No!" he snapped back. "I lost my reputation because I *wasn't* willing to hurt you. I was a son of bitch and I'd done a lot of bad stuff. But never to one of my own. That was the line, and I wasn't gonna cross it, not for anyone. And anyone else who tried was gonna have a problem on their hands. You think all of a sudden, I changed my mind about that? No, Frankie. No."

He pursed his lips, giving his head a disgusted shake. Frank had affronted his honor. "I wanted to tell you all about what you cost me. Having to shove tranquilizers up horses' asses. Losing my position and all that. How the exes didn't care that my income went down, that they still wanted the same alimony and child support. How I got laughed at and didn't get a lick of respect until old Joey in there…" He broke off, taking a steadying breath. "You know, 'til he wasn't around anymore. Only then did I get back to where I was. I wanted to make you feel bad, wanted an apology."

Carlo looked away again, swallowing hard. "So, I followed you when I saw you pull out of the parking lot. You stopped right behind me just before I pulled out to follow, you know. Freaked me out. You stopped right behind me and stared at my car. I thought you recognized me. But I guess not. You kept driving. And I pulled out then and followed you."

The Genesis. Carlo had been the one in the Genesis that he and Bianca had been staring at. Frank's mouth fell open, his clouded mind trying to remember that day without focusing on Bianca and the way she'd screamed at the sight of the truck.

But what did Carlo have to do with the accident? It was not as if he'd been driving the truck.

"I don't know what happened," Carlo said, shaking his head. "I was trying to keep up and I turned the wrong way down a one-way street. Not a big deal you know. It happens. I was the only one driving on it. But when I pulled out onto the two-way… there was a truck. And we both swerved to avoid running into each other…" He swallowed again. "And I don't remember what happened after that."

Frank did. He knew exactly what had happened.

The truck that had so violently t-boned his car had been driving on the wrong side of the road. It's why he didn't see him coming.

And now he knew for certain what had caused the driver to act like that. The driver had to veer into the opposing traffic to avoid another car. Carlo's car.

And then the truck drove straight into Frank's vehicle instead, killing Bianca.

"It was just that important to talk to me, huh?" he seethed, looking into his lap, feeling both angry and numb simultaneously. Anger at Carlo's hand in what had happened, numb from the drugs, and maybe a weird sort of acceptance that it was still just one of those things.

That no one had set out to hurt his family that day but had anyway.

The news left him wrestling with his emotions. *So, would it have been better if a stranger had pulled out in front of the truck? Would I be more or less forgiving?*

"I'm sorry, Frankie. I wish I could come up with better words to tell you how sorry I am. How I'll never stop being sorry for what I done. To you and a lot of other people."

Frank wanted more than anything to stand up, to pace back and forth, just to put some space between him and Carlo's massive shoulders, which brushed against his intermittently as they talked. But he didn't trust himself to stand up quickly. Trusted himself even less to walk for any distance or length of time.

"I did see you in the hospital, didn't I?" he asked.

Carlo nodded, staunching his cigar straight on the concrete table. "Probably. I don't remember. I'd had a custom steering wheel put on that car. Don't like the new ones, you know; they're too small. So, I'd got a big one put on…" He held his hands up, shoulder-width apart. "Did a number on my head."

Yeah, it did. I saw that clear as day. Seen it twice now.

"I shouldn't have been driving at all, Frankie. I should have stayed on my blood pressure pills. I should have…" He sighed, shaking his head angrily. "I should have listened to you. All those years ago. I could have done anything. And this is what I chose. Just because I thought my old man was cool. And I wanted to be cool too. Every kid wants to be just like his old pop."

Well, I didn't, thought Frank.

Even with the booze and the pills, Frank's heart pounded in his ears as he stared at Carlo—the boy he'd looked up to, who grew up to be the man you knew you shouldn't screw with.

Now though, Frank just found himself looking at a sad old man full of nothing but regrets, sitting there telling him he was the reason his life had ended that day.

The reason Bianca is dead…

"Maybe it would be cool if I just killed you now?"

The words slithered out of Frank's mouth before he could stop them, but he found he wasn't sorry. He let his stare burn into Carlo's face, surprised not to see an angry reaction there. If anything, he relaxed, leaning back and crossing his ankle over his knee.

"Not your style, Frankie boy. Never was," he said with an air of resignation. "That's why you're going where you're going. And I'm not heading there with you. Not now, not ever."

Grinding his jaw, Frank swallowed hard, knowing the truth of it. He had fought many times in life, never willing to let anyone push him around.

But he'd never once done violence out of revenge. But that didn't make him special. It wasn't even because of his own morality. If it hadn't been for Bianca, Frank thought maybe he would have jumped headlong into the 'mob associate' lifestyle.

Maybe he would have decided he was a tough guy too, telling himself the whole time that he was morally superior to the actual mobsters but living it up with the dirty money they paid him.

He'd been headed that way, but Bianca stopped him.

What if she hadn't found out? Or worse, what if he had ignored her?

You're not any better than Carlo. You just had better people around you. The thought was loud in his head, but not in an accusatory tone, just a statement of fact.

And who was to say someone else wouldn't have pulled out in front of that truck? Maybe it was just Bianca's day. His day. Carlo's day.

Maybe everything in his life had played out exactly as it was supposed to?

Suddenly, Frank noticed how quiet it had become on the patio. Silent, even. Overwhelmingly so. There was no noise coming from inside. Nothing from the alleyway or even the more distant sounds from the street.

It was just quiet.

He blinked rapidly, trying to clear the fog in his head, but it seemed as if the lights had dimmed a bit too. And Carlo seemed farther away than he had been a second ago.

"We all have our roles to play, Frank. There's a lot of routes to walk. And most of the time, you chose the right one. Every once in a while, you needed someone to show you the way. And lucky for you, you always listened. Not like me. I think you were there to show me the way. And I decided not to go with you. I think about that a lot."

Frank nodded. He had always known that Bianca was there to show him the way. The only time he'd ever faltered was when he'd taken another path.

"So, it's only right that it's on me to return the favor." Carlo looked over at him, the fog reflecting off his eyes, giving them a dead look. "Something else you need to know now… this isn't the first time we've had this conversation."

Frank drew back, confused. Maybe Carlo had drunk more than he'd thought.

"This ain't the first time I've had to sit here and tell you I'm the reason Bianca was taken from you. It ain't the first time I've helped you put the pieces together of that day."

"Carlo, what the hell are you talking about?" he whispered, sure his head was screwing with him. Because now when he looked in Carlo's eyes, they were glazed over—like cataracts.

"Frankie, we've ended our night here, every night since the day of the accident. You and me. Right here."

A cold sweat formed at his collar, dripping down his chest as he shook his head. "No, I've been at home. Annabella's been taking care of me…"

"Yeah, she has. But not at home," Carlo said, his voice taking on a liquid sound, like he nodded to cough real bad. "You never woke up, Frankie. Annabella *has* been taking care of you ever since. In the hospital. You never did go back home."

I've talked to her! And Viviana and Daniella too! I was there!

He didn't speak aloud, but Carlo heard him anyway. "They talked to you. You didn't talk to them, Frankie. Not really," he explained. "It's nice your girls are so good to you, but that's probably why you held on. You shoulda been gone. You shoulda gone the same time as me."

A knot forming in his stomach, Frank swallowed hard. "If you're gone, but I'm not… then how are we together?"

"I think you're in between," Carlo said sadly. "Close enough to still hear Annabella. But close enough for me to get to you too. We've done this so many times. So many last days. I think…" Carlo breathed out a shaky breath. "I think you're part of my punishment. Sitting here every night and telling you my sin. My secret." Carlo continued. "One of 'em, anyway."

A faint echo drifted in from the alley, pulling Frank's attention away from Carlo, whose face had started to sag more than it should. It was a voice though, wasn't it?

"Tonight is different, Frank," Carlo gasped, his reedy voice pulling Frank's attention back.

"What do you mean different?" asked Frank.

Carlo nodded his head at the alleyway, which had filled with fog. "This is usually the point where I tell you why I'm here, and you get up, walk through that gate, and take a left. And that's the last I see of you. Until tomorrow. Then we meet on the boardwalk and start all over again."

"No!" Frank said, his breath catching in his chest. It felt as though something was sitting on his ribcage. "I can't... I can't breathe!"

The voice drifted out of the alley again, this time clearer.

No, it wasn't coming from the alley. From above? Or all around?

"It's all right, Pop. We're all gonna be okay. We're all gonna be fine. You can go home now. You don't need to keep worrying about us."

"Is that...?" He couldn't get the words out. Couldn't do anything but clutch his chest and double over.

Carlo nodded slowly, seeing the final pieces fall into place, obviously glad to see it happen.

"Is that... Annabella?"

CHAPTER 18

Thursday morning.

"I watched my dad pull the slide back on the gun, holding it to the rear so he could peer into the chamber. Any debris stuck in there could mean a jam at best, or a deadly backfire at worse."

Annabella turned the page of the book, looking up at Frank with a mischievous smile. "Remember when Daniella swiped your firing pin that one time? You were so mad."

There was no answer from her father. No reaction. He lay still in his hospital bed, the beeping of the heartbeat monitor continuing apace, the huff of the ventilator sounding rhythmically.

But still, Annabella liked to think he could hear as she read to him.

Just like he used to read to her when she was little.

She'd picked this book because she thought he'd like it. It was about a father—an old-school mobster—who drew his daughter into a life of crime. He seemed to like it if that made sense.

Last night as she read to him, she got to a scene where the daughter character met a new guy, a criminal, the classic bad boy with a heart of gold. It reminded her of Brad.

She started choking up as she read the passages, forced to stop reading.

And Pop's heart rate had sped up. He didn't move, of course.

The doctors had made it pretty clear he wouldn't be moving anymore either. Not after the cardiac arrest that had brought him back to the intensive care unit.

The room was as sterile as a hospital room could be, not like his room in the coma ward. She had done her best to make that one look like home, bringing in items from her parents' place, including Mom's decorative pillows. Pop didn't notice of course, but it made Daniella happy.

It had been hard getting her to visit initially. But after Annabella did the redecorating, her youngest sister was better about coming to check in every once in a while.

Annabella tried not to get mad at her sisters for not being here. They couldn't have known he would take a turn for the worse so quickly.

Last week when they did come, they'd all had a blast, playing cards and catching up with what was going on in their lives. Both Viviana and Daniella had agreed that Annabella should try online dating. Brad had dumped her, after all. But she just couldn't bring herself to do it.

"I think I'll just be a spinster," she'd told them.

It was good to see them again, to pretend to be normal for one day. Pop had laid there in serene fashion, and both Viviana and Daniella had kissed him goodbye.

By the time he'd gone into cardiac arrest, Viviana had been over in Poland visiting her in-laws and Daniella was in Florida with her new girlfriend.

"I could come back," Daniella had offered when Annabella had called. Viviana had said the same thing. But Annabella told them both not to.

They'd both said their goodbyes last week, even if they hadn't known it. Pop was still in the same state; he wouldn't know whether they were there or not, and he wouldn't want them dragging themselves home for no real reason.

Besides, Annabella was the eldest. This—caring for Pop —was her job. No one else's.

Though if she were being honest, if she'd known how bad it would get, she would probably have considered removing him from life support last week. When she hadn't been alone.

"The greatest love is what you do for others. Especially when no one is looking," Mom used to say. And she'd lived that out every day of her life. Mom never took a day off for herself and had always taken care of them even when she'd been sick or tired. She'd taken care of Pop even when he was being an asshole while he was working in Manhattan.

And now it was Annabella's turn to do the hard thing.

Yes, she would take care of Pop as long as he needed her to.

He always got cold at night, but the shivers had been more pronounced these last two days. The nurse had come in and given him some extra blankets to help warm him, which she appreciated. It would be easy to ignore the old man in a coma in favor of the patients who were expected to wake up. But they were always kind, especially Samantha, the southern girl. She'd been Annabella's only real human contact while she'd been here. The only one she had to talk to.

After he'd started seizing, Annabella had found herself praying that God would take him, then chastising herself for such terrible thoughts. But his life had no quality to it anymore.

He was lost; if Pop was still inside that shell of a body on the bed, she could not see him, couldn't reach him, or he her. So, she had signed a do-not-resuscitate order, knowing Pop would have wanted that too. When he coded, the nurses were only keeping him from falling out of bed or hurting himself. They didn't do anything to save his life. They would not try to save him.

But still he hung on.

"He's not ready to go yet," Samantha had told her, holding her hand as she cried.

He wasn't going to go on his own. But he wasn't going to come back to her either.

Which meant the decision of when her dad would leave this Earth was up to her. Something she just couldn't deal with. Not yet.

The hospice representative spoke all about the option to bring Dad home for the end. That dad could pass away peacefully in his own home if she chose. But it would be an hour by ambulance, and there was no guarantee he would last for the whole drive.

So here they were. In the hospital.

Far away from everything that had ever made him happy. But each time she spoke to him, she talked as if he was right there in his own bed, in his own room, back home.

The night after his cardiac arrest, the doctors did some kind of an electrode treatment to stimulate a response. They and the nurses stood around, giving out the faintest glimmer of hope, just waiting, watching for some sign, however minuscule, to come from Frank.

But there was still nothing. What Annabella had thought was quite correct; he was locked away inside and wouldn't be coming back. Couldn't have found his way even if he had wanted to. It was such a struggle; he couldn't have moved a limb for himself.

They had given her the paper to sign right then, the one that would let them unplug the ventilator. But she couldn't sign it. She just couldn't. "We'll leave this with you, darling," a sweet nurse had said, laying a gentle hand on Annabella's arm. "Whatever you decide, it's always the right thing, sweetheart. You will know when or if the time is right. No one's going to make that decision for you, all right? You're all in control of Dad. So, take your time."

So, there she sat, listening to the beeping heart monitor, the paperwork to end his life sitting on the table beside her. Straightening the blanket over her dad, she edged in closer, whispering in his ear, "Just one more day, Pop. I know it's selfish. But I want just one more day with you, okay? Then I'll send you to be with Mom. You always *were* meant to be together."

***

Friday.

A rap on the doorframe woke Annabella with a start, and she groaned as she shifted uncomfortably in the chair in which she'd fallen asleep.

"Samantha?" she asked groggily, blinking to see the coma ward nurse standing in the doorway of the hospital room.

"Hey hon," she said in her thick Alabama accent. She came into the room and laid a hand on Annabella's shoulder, giving it a squeeze. "We all miss you and Mr. Vitale over there. Not the same without you."

Annabella smiled, happy to see Samantha, even under the circumstances.

Over the year her father had been lingering between life and death, she and Samantha had become true friends, exchanging phone numbers within the first month of meeting.

In a way, she felt Pop liked her too. Somehow, his joints seemed to move better when it was Samantha doing his mobility exercises.

"Someone came by your daddy's old room looking for him. A man," Samantha specified, looking down at her with concern. "I wanted to check with you before I brought him over here."

"It's not Brad, is it?" Annabella asked, furrowing her brow in anger.

"Lord no, I woulda hurled that rat bastard right out the window if he had the nerve to show up now." She crossed her arms over her chest, scowling at the thought of Annabella's ex-boyfriend being put out that Annabella wanted to spend time with her dying father. He hadn't even come to her mom's funeral. That self-serving, narcissistic scumbag!

"Fella said his name was Gino something or other. San-win. Sangwin. Something sounding like that. Oh, *Sanguinetti*. And he looks exactly like you'd think someone with that name would. Cute though," Samantha added, raising her eyebrows and chuckling.

"Oh…" Annabella said, a smile lifting the edge of her lips for the first time in weeks. Unwittingly, she sat up straight in the chair, self-consciously running her fingers through her hair. She wasn't brave enough to get up and look in the mirror.

Oh well. He had seen her without makeup before. It would have to do.

"I guess that means online dating's been going well?" Samantha asked, a delighted smile on her face. "I wish you'd have told me."

Annabella shook her head as she stood, trying in vain to pull the wrinkles from her shirt. "No, of course not. Tinder is still the same trainwreck as ever. Gino… he…"

How could she explain?

"His dad was friends with Pop back when I was a teenager. They stopped being friends before I went to college, but I remembered Gino. He made an impression," she said, hoping she wasn't blushing. "In a really weird coincidence, his dad died in the same pile-up as my mom."

The smile dropped from her face, remembering that horrendous day. She had been standing in the middle of Home Goods when the hospital called her cell phone.

They had gotten her number from Mom's emergency information stored on her iPhone.

Annabella remembered the call so perfectly, how she'd even debated not answering it because why would a hospital in Long Island be calling her?

But she *had* answered it, and life was never the same after that. It was a strange thought she'd had once or twice ever since then. The thought that went, *if you hadn't answered the call that day, maybe fate could've taken a different turn. Maybe if you hadn't taken it, they would never have had a chance to tell you Pop was dead, and...* But it was all futile.

Of course, Daddy would have been dead regardless. Taking or declining a call could not alter fate. Nothing could change fate; for all she knew, Pop had always been destined to die right now.

She didn't remember driving the forty-five minutes to get to the hospital on that day.

Nor did she remember parking the car. It all just happened, somehow, in a blur.

All she remembered was charging into the emergency room, begging for someone to tell her something. "Vitale! Bianca and Frank Vitale! Someone, please tell me what's happened!"

And then she had heard a voice behind her. "Hey, that you, Anna Banana?"

And there had been a ghost from her past, standing right before her—Gino Sanguinetti, along with four other men obviously related to him. None were crying, but she could see right through the Italian stoicism, understanding they had been brought here by a phone call just as she was.

And her heart dropped. The false hope she'd been carrying that her parents would be coming back home in a few days fled her body right at that moment. This was serious.

Maybe deadly.

And even though Gino had just been told about Carlo's sudden and violent death due to veering into a pole, he was there to hold her steady while the doctors told her about her mother. And about her father.

Back in the present, "Oh no. That's wild!" marveled Samantha now. "I'm glad you had someone here with you, even if it was a stranger."

"We hadn't seen each other since we were kids. We're around the same age so, you know, we got to talking. It hit him hard when his dad didn't make it. I guess they'd had a falling out…" *over his dad being a gangster.* She didn't want to say that part aloud. Being from the south, she wasn't sure Samantha would understand, or take it in her stride.

"Well, sounds like I should show him in," Samantha said, smiling again, giving her friend one last squeeze on the arm as she left the room.

Annabella nodded and, as soon as Samantha was out of sight, darted into the bathroom to check her reflection. She had just enough time to brush her hair and splash some water on her face before Samantha's voice came echoing in the hall once more.

Drying off, she emerged back into the room just in time to see Gino walking in.

"Hi," she said, her voice catching in her throat at the bouquet of yellow and white roses he held in his arms. He came toward her, but gingerly, tentatively.

"Hey," he said, looking down shyly. Such an expression looked odd on a big guy like him. Gino was a lineman; he spent his days climbing telephone poles for ConEd, and he looked the part. "Look, I hope I'm not intruding. I saw your Facebook thing and your sisters commented that they couldn't come up yet. I just… I don't want to intrude. But I brought you—"

He held up the flowers awkwardly, as if saying, *I'll just leave these and go*. But Annabella had never been so happy to see anyone in her life.

"Gino, they're beautiful and you're not intruding at all," she said, taking the roses from him and setting them on the table next to Pop. "These are lovely. Mom used to love yellow roses."

After placing the roses, she leaned down and whispered, "Pop? Gino brought you some flowers. You know, Carlo's middle son? The one who came for dinner that one time? They're that same yellow like Mom likes. Sunflower shade. They really brighten up your room. It's like an Italian summer in here. Shame he didn't bring any meatballs."

Her dad always had a great sense of humor; he'd have liked that quip.

The steady *beep, beep,* of his heart monitor continued with no interruption, however, and this time, unlike all the times before, his eyes didn't move beneath his lids. Pop did not hear her talking about the flowers, or about their visitor. Pop was moving away, lost in the in between.

She swallowed hard, sadly aware of him moving farther and farther away from her.

"How's he doing?" Gino asked as she stood up and wiped her eyes.

"Not good," she said, shaking her head. "Since going into cardiac arrest, they moved him to the ICU, and he's just… Well, you can see…" She wafted her arm. "He's so far away. But he won't go on his own either. He needs help… needs…something." *Needs me to turn off the machinery* was in her head, but she also couldn't voice that. "Before, there were a couple times he'd just open his eyes and seem to be looking right at me. Especially while I was talking or reading to him. The doctors said things like that were normal. That's why they tape long-term coma patients' eyes shut. But I kept hoping…"

"You thought he'd wake up?" Gino prompted, moving closer to her dad's bedside.

"I really did," she nodded, trying not to cry. "I thought one day, I'd come to visit and he would just be sitting up in bed and I'd have to tell him about Mom. Or maybe I wouldn't. Maybe he would've heard everything while he was in the coma. There were so many times I said to the doctors and the nurses not to talk about Mom being gone. But they still would. They forgot."

She stared down at the bedside table, her gaze resting on those infernal forms again.

The sterile forms waiting for her signature, the ones that would allow the doctors to end Frank Vitale, sending him into the next dimension to be with Mom, in heaven or wherever.

Gino followed her gaze. "I didn't feel lucky at the time," he said, his voice hoarse. "But I'm grateful I didn't have to do that for my dad. I don't know if I could have."

"I thought you didn't… I mean, you never seemed to get on with him. Even when we were kids."

Gino nodded. "The way he treated my ma… it was a problem. He tried to get better though. Toward the end."

That was exactly the way she remembered it too. In the last year, she and Gino had talked over social media quite a bit, but she'd been careful not to prod into his relationship with his dad. Even when they'd last met in person, she'd known enough to tiptoe around the subject.

Their one and only meeting before the day of the accident had been in high school. Her mom had made her help in the kitchen all day, preparing a special dinner for Pop's childhood friend, Carlo Sanguinetti. The evening had started off badly because Carlo, who had said he was coming to dinner alone, had also brought his wife and son along. It was not a good evening.

Luckily, Mom had made enough to feed an army, but it still set her off kilter. Annabella herself had been off balance for another reason: the sight of Carlo, and his wife—whose name she didn't remember—and Gino walking through the door. The youngest of four sons at the time, Gino had smelled like Gucci and moved like a movie star.

She'd immediately blushed at the sight of him, but lucky for her, Viviana was there to whisper in her ear, "Go stick your head in the freezer real quick."

And she had, which cleared the burning red in her ears immediately.

The dinner had been awkward as hell, and it had been nothing to do with her teenage hormones. Gino's mom was like a cartoon character, a stereotype of the trashy Italian lady showing too much cleavage and saying everything she shouldn't.

And she'd even stained Mom's expensive linen napkins with her bright red lipstick.

As for Carlo though… he was funny, but in a way that was too loud, too vulgar. And she could feel the tension coming from her parents.

Viviana asked to be excused right after the pasta. It was allowed. And after the scaloppine, Gino had stood up and announced, bold as brass, "Ma, I'm gonna go for a walk, okay?" And then he had looked over at Annabella and asked, "You wanna come too?"

Flustered but thrilled, she'd looked over at Mom, pleadingly, bolting out of her seat upon getting a resigned nod.

"Don't go past the end of the block," Pop had called after her.

The second they were out the door, Gino had immediately done two things: whipped off his jacket and placed it over Annabella's shoulders, then pulled out a pack of cigarettes from his jeans pocket. "God, my mom is so embarrassing!" he'd grumbled, tapping out a cigarette from the pack, lighting it, then passing it to her in one fluid move.

She didn't smoke, but she wasn't going to pass up a chance to put her mouth on the cigarette he had just lit for her. He was the cutest boy ever to have spared her a second glance. And even though it was cringe-inducing watching her mom and his mom interact, she was so glad he'd come over. And she really hoped he would again.

She dutifully took a puff on the cigarette, but did not inhale it.

She blew out all the smoke as she passed the cigarette back to him.

"Is your dad really in the mob?" she asked.

"I'm not supposed to say," he replied casually, taking another drag as they walked slowly toward the end of the block. His hesitance was an obvious affirmative.

"Does that mean *my* dad's in the mob too?" she blurted out, unsure she even wanted to know.

That made him laugh. "Nah. People like my dad, they only cling to people like your dad so they can pretend to be normal! So don't worry 'bout that."

For some reason, that made her feel good. "I get that."

Everyone wanted to feel normal. Even mobsters. And it made her feel good that her dad was the type of person that a mafia guy would look up to. Odd but true.

She was definitely happy about the prospect that Gino should soon be making regular appearances at her dinner table.

But that hadn't turned out to be the case.

Instead, that night of walking under the stars and pretending to smoke a cigarette with the handsomest boy she'd ever seen had been her one and only conversation with him. The only time she got to have his cologne-infused coat draped over her shoulders. And since he lived all the way over in Brooklyn, it wasn't as if their paths would ever cross naturally.

Then, something peculiar happened; their dads had suddenly and without explanation stopped being friends. And Annabella had gotten on with her life, found other boys to be besotted with. Until, twenty years later, a horrible accident brought them both to the same emergency room.

She had sat with him, holding his hand that day as he processed the death of his father. And in turn, he would have considered that he was sitting with her to console the loss of her mother, and the grievous injuries of her father. They had one another, and it felt better.

Now, so much later and completely without prompting, he had come here to console her again. It seemed oddly incongruous, the mobster's boy coming to aid a girl at her lowest ebb.

"You gonna wait for your sisters? To sign?" he asked, looking across at the forms.

She shook her head. "Viviana's in Poland with her in-laws. And Daniella, that's my little sister, she's in Florida. And honestly… I feel like she doesn't want to come."

Gino shook his head, laying a hand on her arm.

"Hey, you know that ain't true. My youngest brother didn't come to the hospital for my dad either and it wasn't because he didn't love him. Hell, he was Pop's favorite. 'Ah, my boy making money off video game nerds.' He used to go on and on about him. I mean, yeah, the kid's done good for himself. Not old enough to drink and he bought himself a brownstone. More glamorous than a guy working for ConEd," he said in a rueful manner.

Better that than what your brothers do.

She didn't say it aloud. And she didn't pry.

But she was certain at least one of his brothers was in the mob and thought maybe he'd done time for it. She didn't have any criminals in the family but it had to be so hard for the kids.

"Anyway," Gino said. "Not everyone has the strength to do the necessary. Some can barely deal with their own grief. And guilt. Don't think your sister doesn't care. I bet she does. A lot."

Annabella nodded, amazed how he could know Daniella so well even though he'd never even met her. She had always been the most emotional, the one least able to handle those emotions. Annabella had been out of the house when Daniella really started acting up, but she knew it had been a huge problem for Mom and Pop.

Maybe she felt guilty about it now. For stealing precious time away from Pop.

She hoped not.

Annabella looked at Gino, flicking her eyes at the forms.

"I'm a… I'm going to call the nurse. I told them I would do it today."

She barely got through the sentence as a sob choked her throat, and she looked down, not wanting to make Gino uncomfortable.

"You want me to go?" he asked.

Part of her wanted to tell him yes, just so he wouldn't have to be saddled with her grief. He had his own to deal with and she didn't want to be a burden.

But her father's voice came back, saying, "Don't shoo people away when they're trying to take care of you, honey," Pop had told her once. "Let someone else be brave sometimes too. It can't always be you, my beautiful strong girl."

"Would you mind staying?" she asked, barely able to whisper through the tears.

"I wouldn't mind at all," he said, looking into her eyes.

And it was clear he meant every word of it, grateful to share the moment.

Together, they sat at Pop's bedside, Annabella holding Frank's hand as the nurse—one whose name she didn't know—quietly and without fuss disconnected the ventilator, turning off the machines one by one. "All done now, love," the nurse said. "I'll leave you with Dad. We're only outside, Annabella, so come get any one of us nurses when you need us."

She nodded slightly, staring at Frank's lined face, longing to see one last flicker of emotion, a sign that he knew she was there. But there was nothing, just his labored, unassisted breaths on the air. It was so hard to say goodbye, but at least this time, she had that opportunity, one she would appreciate in the future when she was making peace with herself.

She hadn't had the opportunity to say goodbye to Mom, hadn't been given time to tell her how much she was loved one last time.

At least with Pop, she had been able to. Maybe this way wasn't so terrible.

"It's all right, Pop. We're all gonna be okay. We're all gonna be fine. You can go home now. You don't need to worry about us all anymore; we're all grown women. Were fine, and we always will be fine. And besides, you'll watch over us from the next place. With Mom."

With one final great gasp, Frank Vitale breathed his last breath.

And though Gino believed she had imagined it, Annabella reported being sure she had seen him smile. Gino would never tell her otherwise.

EPILOGUE

The weight on Frank's chest evaporated. The pain, the tightness in his body. It was all gone. He could take a full breath for the first time in what seemed like forever.

Frank snapped his head to look at Carlo, not understanding what had just happened.

"You see, Frank, that exit door at the bar never had any sign on it before. But tonight, it says, 'Paradiso.' So, this really was your last day. Here is where we part, pal."

Carlo rotated in his seat and jerked his head toward the gate. "You wanna go that way. Through the gate and to the right."

Frank turned his body likewise, only just realizing the fog wasn't in his head, but all around him, parting in a near-perfect path to the wrought iron gate that would lead him out of the patio and into the alleyway.

He nodded, realizing Carlo was ending their night together.

He'd told him all he needed to tell him.

And now Carlo understood it was time for Frank to do what he needed to do.

The edge of Frank's mouth lifting just slightly, he stood up carefully, placing one hand on Carlo's shoulder and the other in his pocket where the bottle of pills was.

"You gonna stay here?" he asked him, not wanting Carlo to go back into the bar with Joey and the rest of those creeps after he'd gone.

He nodded, looking down to hide the shine in his eyes.

"For a while longer. I don't get to go yet."

Frank squeezed his shoulder, starting to shuffle toward the gate, careful to keep his balance. Turning back one last time to where Carlo sat alone at the table, he called, "I'll see you."

"I hope so."

Frank reached out, grabbing onto the cold metal of the gate, lifting the handle. It stuck for a moment, but then gave way, the rusted metal lifting up off the latch, the gate swinging open.

Frank stepped out into the alleyway, looking first to his left, where the fog was so thick, he could barely see two feet ahead. Then he turned to the right, where the air was clear. Not a hint of fog in sight, just a clear night, the streetlights shining from the end of the alley.

Funny how that works, he thought, turning right, heading toward the street.

Stepping around the last dumpster, Frank emerged onto the street, a one-way two-laner with cars parked on either side, but no traffic. All the buildings had their lights turned out, even on the upper levels where no doubt there were lofts, and apartments.

But tonight, on this street, no one was up and moving but him.

… or so he thought.

A movement out of the corner of his eye drew his attention.

He snapped his head around, noticing that all the wooziness from the pills and drinks had completely worn off. His head was clear. No dizziness at all. He felt like a young man again.

With the renewed focus in his sight, he caught a glimpse of a woman walking away from him, her green, calf-length dress swaying with every step, her glossy brunette hair pinned up neatly, but still shining in the streetlamps as she passed.

"Bianca?" he whispered, turning to go after her.

It was her, he was sure of it, and he picked up the pace, moving faster than he'd dared all day.

Nearly running, he crossed the street, thinking of calling out, but holding off. What if it wasn't her? How would that look? Would it spook her? Would he appear like some pervert?

It would probably scare her to death, seeing some crazy man running after her in the street. That was the last thing he wanted to do. But soon, he had come within throwing distance of her, slowing and squinting, trying to get a better look without being a full-on creep and grabbing her, spinning her around.

The woman stopped in her tracks, jolting Frank to a stop too. He'd been too loud.

Somewhere, a loud gong sounded, then another, a clock striking twelve. It was midnight.

The woman in front turned to face him.

"Bianca?" he whispered, his eyes filling at the sight of his beautiful wife, looking just as she had on the day he'd first seen her on the bus.

She smiled, holding out her hand.

"There you are, you silly man. The day's over, honey. It's time to go home."

Frank reached out and took Bianca's hand, overcome with joy and relief. "Yes, we should go home now."

He had kept her waiting long enough.